Vampires of Nirvana
Book 2
Point Of No Return

Ranay James

Copyright 2015 Ranay James

Ranay James
1209 South Main Street
#126
Lindale, Texas 75771
www.ranayjames.com

Publishers Note: This is a work of fiction. Names, characters, places and incidents are a product of the author's imagination. Locales and public names are sometimes used for atmospheric purposes. Any resemblance to actual people, living or dead, or to businesses, companies, events, institutions, or locales is completely coincidental.

Vampires of Nirvana: Book 2 Point Of No Return — 1st ed.
ISBN 978-0-9967862-2-5

Other Series By Ranay James

Series by Ranay James available in e-book format at all major retailers through the following website:

WWW.booklaunch.io/ranayjames

The McKinnon Legends A Time Travel Series

The McKinnon American Men A Romantic Suspense Series

Vampires Of Nirvana is a ten part series that with each book will leave you begging for more. If you love the McKinnons, then you are going to love the royal family of Nirvana.

Print Editions Available:

Vampires of Nirvana: Book 1- Never Kiss Me Goodbye
Vampires of Nirvana: Book 2 - Point of No Return
The McKinnon The Beginning: Book One Part 1
The McKinnon The Beginning: Book One Part 2
Unfinished Business: Book Two Part 1
Unfinished Business: Book Two Part 2

Audiobook Editions:
Available at Audiobooks.com and Audible.com
The McKinnon The Beginning: Book One Parts 1 and 2
Unfinished Business: Book Two Parts 1 and 2
The McKinnon Legends Books One and Two: Parts 1 & 2

The McKinnon The Beginning Book One Part 1
The McKinnon The Beginning Book One Part 2
Unfinished Business Book Two Part 1
Unfinished Business Book Two Part 2

To my husband—thank you for being my partner through life and supporting my dreams.

I have been impressed with the urgency of doing. Knowing is not enough; we must apply. Being willing is not enough; we must do.

—LEONARDO DA VINCI

Chapter 1

Southern Caribbean
McKinnon Private Retreat

It had been three weeks since that night in Dallas when Slade almost lost Kristen. He elected not to think of that night. It was better that way. Their cover had been blown sky-high right along with the cottage leaving them little choice but to flee. It was the only way to allow her recovery to happen in peace and quiet.

Chase had suggested this retreat, so after being granted an extension to his reporting date to Broken Arrow, Slade found himself still neck deep in Kristen's security detail.

Who would ever think to look for her in the Caribbean, Slade thought. The last few days had been something of an experience for him. She was emerging as a force of nature now that the initial shock of Kari's death was passing.

He found it to be her way to push that tragedy behind her. She was strong, resilient, and amazingly tough. Her mind was sharp, her humor boundless, and her powers of observation acute. She was a constant source of entertainment for them all, keeping them laughing and thoroughly relaxed.

Slade was the exception.

She was like a hurricane, ripping a wide path of destruction across his defenses. She was high octane, sweeping through his life with a force to be dealt with carefully, and plenty of avoidance was in order.

That tactic of avoidance was the only way to keep from giving into his desire to sleep with her. As long as there were others around he was fine, but she kept asking him to spend time together one-on-one, and that could never happen.

Kristen was pacing like a caged animal. "I'm going crazy!"

Slade felt for her. "Just be patient a few more days, baby. I'm sure we can get you home. The last time I talked to Detective Lacy, he had made some excellent progress. I put him onto the leads of the unusual permitting. It is just too bad the disk I copied in New Mexico never showed up, and the original was destroyed in the explosion. I'm sure there was more there we could have utilized if we had been given the opportunity to look it over more thoroughly."

"How is it you can continue to work and I can't? It's just not fair," she protested softly. "Do you realize, Jericho, how crazy this is making me? And do you realize how bad the work and the responsibilities back home are piling up because I'm a pampered prisoner in this lovely paradise?" She spread her arms out wide referring to the lovely villa on the very exclusive, privately owned island of Turtle Shell Cay. It was totally self-sufficient and totally off the grid. The only way in, out, on, or off was by boat or small aircraft.

Slade hid his smile, understanding this was hard on her. "It's a different kind of work. And I don't think of my responsibility to you as work, Kristen. So just relax. This lull may be the only opportunity you have to let yourself begin to heal. Just enjoy yourself," he advised.

Slade looked at the sling she was sporting. The explosion had sent her to the ground hard enough that it had almost broken her arm. The fall severely sprained it. He and Chase agreed that leaving some injury was necessary, regardless of the fact he wanted to leave her fully free of any pain. It was the only wound he left and the only one she remembered. Otherwise, she would never believe she had not sustained some damage. He had seen to it that he wiped her mind completely clean of the rest. He just hoped the sweep stuck.

Too bad he couldn't do the same with his memories.

He hadn't had a decent night's sleep since he emerged from her. He would sleep until the dreams would jolt him awake with searing intensity. One unexpected byproduct of his time inside her was he could see her dreams. The things she was letting him do to her in those dreams were criminal in several states, and what she was doing to his insides had to be illegal in several more.

He always seemed to find himself standing by her bed each night unable to leave her side. He could never crawl in that bed and stay either. As a result, he usually spent his nights power-napping in a chair in the far corner of her room or taking watch just sitting on the bed next to her, leaning his back against the headboard while sitting on top of the covers. On the nights that it was really appalling, he had to get Chase to take watch. Those nights he went to the gym and worked out to the point of exhaustion.

He continued to argue his case as he sat at the kitchen bar in the open-air villa and watched her wear a hole in the Italian marble floor.

"Will you just sit down and relax? It's warm, the weather is fantastic, and we have a butler and a chef waiting on us hand and foot."

"So what if we do?" She shrugged before going on further. "Slade, I don't need a chef or a butler. I need to work."

What she was trying to tell him was when it all boiled down was that she needed something constructive to direct her time and energies. She needed something to distract her. She needed something monotonous, tedious and challenging, something demanding her total focus. Ever since he had slammed that door to the cottage, she was in a state of arousal of varying degrees nearly every waking moment. Just like him. Her nights were even worse. Just like his.

She needed some relief—relief he couldn't give her.

He was having second thoughts about any personal contact between them, and no amount of teasing, flirting, or enticing would work. She had said that morning that short of walking naked into his room and crawling into bed with him, she was at a loss as to how to gain his attention. She accused him of being as immovable and as impervious to her as fortress walls. Short of treachery, he was not going to be breached. And, as a result, neither was she. And though he found her metaphor witty, and he understood her frustration it changed nothing.

Slade saw her faraway look, and the small smile playing at the corners of her mouth and wondered if she was thinking about last night at the pool. He had watched from the window and breathed a sigh of relief when she said no to Chase. He was very glad that he didn't have to see just how firm his resolve was to let her go. He came close to pulling his gun and shooting Chase in the back when he had come up from behind her.

Maybe he was leaving her to her own designs too much lately. That little guiding voice where she was concerned was silent of late. It left him winging it.

"I watched you swimming last night," Slade confessed.

Kristen was surprised as she momentarily stopped her pacing. "Chase was just being Chase, Slade. Nothing is going on between us." She waved the idea away. Just the night before, after they had eaten, she asked Slade to go for a swim with her. He swiftly declined just as he had the three previous nights and then like a coward, which she had called him, he proceeded to lock himself away in the game room doubling as an office.

She put on her suit nevertheless and dove in for a few laps on her own, hoping to work off some pent-up energy that had been building from the inactivity. After a half hour, Chase came outside to join her for a cooling dip in the infinity pool.

At the time she was standing at the far end looking up at the night sky, marveling at the stars so vivid this far away from city lights. Chase had silently slipped up behind her and placed his palms on her hips.

"Beautiful, aren't they?" he had asked, pulling her ever more slightly against him.

"Very," she said, briefly looking over her shoulder at him before returning her gaze to the heavens. "I've never seen anything shine so brightly."

He turned her around to look at him. "Neither have I."

For a moment, she had seen something deep there inside him. For all his lighter side, there was a very complicated man hidden away from most eyes to see. However, she was a master at reading people. It was what she did for a living. She seldom saw him completely sober. So, his next question had surprised her. That surprise was not so much that he asked. It was that he was deadly serious.

"Kris, come clean with me. How much discomfort are you in?"

"I'm good, Chase. My arm feels fine."

He had paused, studying her with those cool green eyes. "Tsk tsk, you disappoint me, Doctor Ransom." He shook his head in mock displeasure, back to his usual character. "Your nooossse is grooowwwing." His sing-song statement accompanied a tweak on her nose, and there was nothing overtly sexual about the single fingertip that he slid down her collarbone. That small physical contact caused her to involuntarily suck in a lung full of air.

"You, lady, are so busted," he had softly and wickedly laughed.

"Ok, so maybe a little." The confession had certainly hurt.

"Now, we're getting somewhere with this diagnosis," he had continued to tease. "If you were a dude, I'd tell you to take a cold shower and call me in the morning. However, you're *definitely* not a dude, so more drastic measures are in order, I'm afraid," he said, sighing heavily.

To his credit, Chase graciously and humbly offered the cure for her disease in the form of himself as the antidote, "as a selfless act of personal sacrifice, I lay upon the altar," as he put it.

For all his horsing around, she knew he was not joking with the offer. He understood women better than any man she had ever encountered. It wasn't that he had a feminine

8

side, leading to common understanding and empathy. He just had the gift with women, and he was sensing her compelling need. He was fully confident that he could help her. If she were of any other disposition, it would be more than tempting. However, at this point, she had it under control, barely but still under control, and did not need the complication. He liked her. He didn't love her, though, and, unlike her, he could compartmentalize the act. He would detach it from his emotional side, choosing to look at it just as he said: the antidote and a way to get her physical relief much like a prescription cream for an itchy rash.

She had laughed, thanking him for his most gallant offer of self-sacrifice and then declined.

He had placed his hand over his heart in mock rejection, rolled his eyes back in his head, and then fell backward into the deep end of the pool. She impulsively jumped in behind him, and for the next few minutes, they splashed water at each other, resulting in a fun bout of dunking and seeing who could hold their breath the longest underwater. She won the bet, so he had to take her fishing. She suspected that he let her win.

Laughing at his antics had helped for a few minutes and just proved her point that she needed a distraction. She needed to work.

Slade has to know that, she thought.

Slade defended voicing his observation. "I never said there was anything between the two of you. That wasn't why I mentioned it." Yes, it was, he admitted in his mind after the fact. He did it subconsciously to see her reaction. "Let me see your arm."

She stepped closer, removing her arm before pulling the sling over her head. Slade took the sling from her hand and laid it to the side. He reached over for her arm, extended it, pulled it, all the while checking for flexibility. "Does it hurt when I do this?" he asked, slightly twisting and lifting it out to the side.

She shook her head. In truth, she did feel good. Other than a mild discomfort still lingering in her arm, she felt better than she had in years. Her energy levels were skyrocketing, her skin and hair looked healthier than it ever had, and for the first time since her escape from the pimp, she had no pain in her lower abdomen from the scar tissue that riddled her. At first, she just chalked it up to the pain meds Slade was cramming down her throat. However, she had stopped taking those days ago.

"I think your arm is up to it. Let me take you diving today out by the reef."

"You're a diver?" She was genuinely surprised.

"Why the surprise?" he asked with a small laugh, cocking his head to the side.

"Hello? Duh! You live in Arizona, Slade."

Residing in Arizona would not usually lend itself to becoming a diver. For Kristen, Slade had proven to be a basket full of surprises over the last three weeks. She was beginning to believe the things Slade did in his spare time were just as dangerous, if not more so than the things he did on the job with the police force.

"I dive up at the Hoover Dam and Lake Mead all the time. See, I'm not totally the job," he teased. It was a lie but who was she to argue? If she tossed that stone in the glass house in which she was living, there would be several broken windows to repair, he mused.

She stopped the pacing she had resumed and just raised one brow in question as if to say she had his number. "And let me guess, Diver Dan... It's rescue and recovery diving that you do, and recreation has squat to do with it."

He laughed. "Yeah, ok, so you got me there, but it's still diving." He shrugged and winked. "Right?"

"Slade, why don't you just admit it? Just like me, you're a lost cause when it comes to work, which, by the way, is something I'm currently not getting done thanks to you and that walking live oak friend of yours." She tossed her head to the side indicating Chase, who was currently lounging by the pool, and on the side table next to him, the butt of his gun was not as cleanly hidden as he might think. *Maybe we all are "the job,"* she pondered.

Slade smiled. The last few days had been a mixed treat for him. She was looking better and feeling stronger, and her sense of humor was returning. The problem was he was losing the battle with himself. No longer having the excuse of her being on the injured reserve listing, his desires were beginning to wear on him. There was nothing to keep that small voice in his head at bay. He wanted her in a way that twisted his inside, and the longer he didn't act, the more aggressive Chase was becoming with her.

And Kristen's actions towards him were no longer subtle, either.

She would come up behind him while he was working and put her arms around his neck, looking over his shoulder, and ask him what he was doing, but the one that was truly killing him was her new nightly habit.

Having absolutely no regard for the closed door of his room, she simply waltzed in unannounced and crawled on the bed beside him in the evenings as he watched television or did work on his laptop. It didn't matter if he locked the door or not. She had figured out how to unlock it from the hallway. She would bring him a cold glass of tea just how he liked it, hand it to him, and without a word, she would settle in. As long as he would stay put, she would simply run her fingers through his hair as she leaned up against the headboard. It was the only physical contact between them, and it was driving him crazy. Slade had debated cutting his hair, thinking it might stop this little ritual. However, he had yet to follow through. She said she liked it long and who was he kidding?

Slade thought she glowed with health and vibrancy. He also realized she was glowing because she was a hollaquine, finally seeing with open eyes what had been there all along. Just under the surface, a shimmer was enhanced by the tropical sun. If he could bottle that glow, he would be a millionaire a hundred times over. Much more of her and he would be violating a second personal code: never mix business with pleasure. After the explosion, he renewed his vow to keep it professional before he managed to get her killed through his inattention brought on by her being a heady distraction.

"Speaking of work," he said, reaching for the satellite phone, "I need to make a call and then we can go on that dive."

Slade called Detective Lacy to see if Detective Green had ever shown up for duty. Green could be a prick and pain in the ass, but it was unlike the veteran cop not to be at work. They had made several calls to his house, and no one answered. He was now officially a missing person. He may not have always liked Green, but he was a fellow officer, and it concerned him that Green was AWOL. Just like him, Green had touched both the senator's case, and Kari's, and that common thread was now, even more, important. Slade was on the speaker using his hands to check the condition of his mask, dive computer, and regulator.

"He still hasn't checked in?" Slade stopped in mid-motion of resetting the controls of his dive computer. He pulled his brows together.

Kristen pulled out a stool and sat down at the bar next to him, her leg touching his, and absently fingered the diving gear without really thinking about it.

"Not a word," Lacy replied. "No one has seen him since he went back to interview that grandson who supposedly is living in the apartment below the Ransom girl's apartment."

Slade could hear the familiar police department noises in the background. He was finding Kristen's prediction to be correct. He was missing the work way more than he thought possible.

Up till now keeping her safe had kept him busy up until the last couple of days.

He saw that a hobby was definitely in order.

He wasn't like Chase, who would be happy doing almost nothing as long as it involved a woman and one of his three favorite boys: José Cuervo, Jim Beam, or Johnny Walker. Chase had two speeds—full throttle or park.

Slade sucked at downtime almost as much as Kristen did. She needed a dose of her own advice on getting a hobby. Apparently, the two of them only had one speed, and that was called drive.

"What did he gain from the interview or did we even get his notes?" Slade asked. Without thinking, he reached across the granite countertop, bringing her fingers to his lips and unaware of the gesture being too distracted with the conversation. Sitting there with him, this was the first time he had reached out to touch her in a purely affectionate way since they arrived.

"Never got 'em. I've gone back to the apartment, but there is no grandson and no grandmother. The apartment is empty. The landlord denies having a lease on the apartment. He claims he was doing a major remodel after the last tenant caught the kitchen on fire. It seems that it has been vacant for over six months."

"Did you verify?" Slade asked, intertwining his fingers with hers. She leaned over taking advantage of his receptiveness and rested the side of her head on his shoulder.

"Yeah, there were still some painter's ladders and miscellaneous tools left around, however, nothing in the way of personal items. There was cat hair everywhere, but that could mean Kari's cat paid the apartment a visit on a routine basis."

All right, Slade thought. Maybe one of the contractors had a key to the vacant apartment and just let himself in and used the fire escape to get into Kari's place. It was another possibility. Kari's cat was still another.

However, it did not compute that the shifter would kill his benefactor. According to Kristen, Kari had Bobby for at least a year. Too bad Slade could not get his hands on him. The shifter would undoubtedly have information and may even be able to pinpoint the killer.

"Find the contractors and interview them. Watch your back, Lacy. From what the chief said yesterday, Powell and Foster were almost ambushed."

"It could just be coincidence, Slade. It was a dicey neighborhood."

"Still…" Slade let the warning hang.

"I know. With Green missing, I'm now the detective on record, and it is looking like anyone who touches this case is a potential target."

"Yeah, something like that. Just watch your six."

"I guess you called it, Slade."

"Called what?" Slade asked, absently stroking Kristen's hair as she leaned her head on his shoulder.

"We all heard you and the chief make that bet that the Ransom girl would end up dead from her reporting."

Kristen sat up and went deadly still beside him.

Slade groaned, closing his eyes and drawing his fingertips across his forehead. He understood how Kris would take that comment. He scrunched up his face as he darted his eyes over at her.

Could she read his body language? He was ashamed and concerned. Still, it probably wouldn't change things for her.

Her look was full of hurt, anger, and disgust all rolled into one when she looked Slade's direction. Slowly, she pulled her hand from his. "Slade, is this true?"

She waited for him to deny it, he could see that. His silence was answer enough and damning in her eyes.

"You felt she was in danger, placed a bet on her life, and did nothing to protect her?"

He sighed heavily and watched her get up from the bar to walk out. She stopped before fully leaving the room, having one more thing to say. "You sorry, cold-blooded bastard. You might as well have killed her yourself."

"Kristen?" He didn't say anymore knowing she wasn't listening.

Lacy apologized. "Sorry, man. I should have known the walls have ears."

"It's done, and we can't unring that bell. Just watch your back and let me know if Green surfaces," Slade said, watching her over his shoulder as she walked away. He heard her climbing the stairs going to the bedrooms. She turned right at the top of the stairs instead of left. She was going to her room, not to his.

He hung up the phone and went to do damage control.

Chapter 2

Kristen was hurt. She thought she understood Slade. Once again, Kristen had misjudged a man. Was it any wonder she was still single? She had thought and felt somehow he was different.

"I am different," he mumbled softly. He could feel and hear every one of her thoughts.

Unfortunately, she was still floating inside him and one by-product he quickly discovered upon her reviving at the cabin was that he could hear her strongest emotional thoughts and see all her dreams. The side effect was fading but not fast enough to suit him. He hated to think what she would do if she realized her every strong waking thought and some not-so-awake thoughts and dreams were playing across his mind like a very disjointed movie that had no end. It was driving him to distraction, especially when she focused on two things: him and how she felt, and it appeared that what she felt was scorching hot and sensual.

Her dreams kept him awake and in the shower, a lot.

The second topic was, even more, disheartening.

She kept wondering why she was not attractive to him. There was no way he could tell her she was the most beautiful thing he had ever seen or felt in his life. He would only break her heart. She was in love with him. He felt that. How could he not? Still he couldn't make her his woman no matter how much he might want her.

He had made a choice to heal her. He would continue to stand by that decision.

He could save her but never have her. It was worth his sacrifice to know she was still alive.

Slade lightly knocked on the closed door. It tore at him as he felt and heard the thoughts and feelings ripping a hole in her. He had disappointed her, and let her down emotionally. She needed him both physically and emotionally, and he was pushing her away. She had no idea why, seeing no real obstacle to their being together, even if for just a short time until he had to report in Broken Arrow.

How did he tell her that it wasn't her? He was the issue and would love nothing better than to crawl back inside her?

"Kristen, baby, I'm sorry. It wasn't a real wager. You have to try to understand that death is something we homicide cops deal with every day."

She spoke softly, standing just on the other side of that door, resting her forehead on the highly polished teakwood. "So you joke and make bets, and I'm supposed to be fine with that?"

"No, no, I'm not saying you should be okay with it. I'm just saying that maybe, sometimes, I might be insensitive because of that overexposure. I freely admit it was crass and tactless. And I'm sorry I said it and that you had to hear I did."

She pulled the door open unexpectedly, causing him to take a step back. She took full advantage of the gap.

"Kris, where do you think you are going?" he asked as she pushed past him and made for the front door.

"I forgive you, but I need space, Slade. I feel smothered."

Never breaking her stride, she bounded down the terrazzo tile steps to the crushed coral and shell driveway and past the small golf cart. Her steps crunched underfoot as she walked away from the villa. The sun continued its rise high and intense in the late morning sky.

"I'll go with you." He followed.

She wheeled, holding up her hands as if to stop him from advancing any farther. "For God's sake just give me some breathing room! Just please... leave me alone." She

21

desperately needed space. "I'm on an island in the middle of the Caribbean. It's not like I can walk away from you. And I'm not sure you wouldn't welcome the distance. I seem just to be underfoot for you lately. If you don't want to be around me, you should have never taken the job."

"That's a cheap shot, Kris. It's not true, and you know it."

She paused, taking a deep breath and letting it out before finishing. "Look, Slade, I just need some space. I feel like you're in my head as it is." She paused to collect her thoughts. "I'm not sure what's happening, and I can't make out the words. It is more like a buzz that I can never escape. It's making me crazy."

"I'm sorry, Kris." He was sorry that she was going through all this and sorry that she had to hear about the bet.

"I've already forgiven you, because I understand, Slade. You have your guilt to bear because that wager has proven so prophetic. I'm not going to add to that by holding a grudge."

"Thank you for that. Will you come back to the villa?"

"No, Slade, please, just let me go."

The soft words hit him deep. He paused before nodding his consent, wondering just how literal her words actually might be.

She turned and hadn't taken three steps before he stopped her.

"Wait a minute. Here," he said, and, reaching inside the golf cart, he got her sun hat and placed it on her head. "Don't take it off." And with that, he let her go. If she needed a little breathing room, then what else could he do? However, he was not about to leave her uncovered, her head or her body. Before she got very far, he silently gave the command for the other two bodyguards to follow. With his hands, he signaled to give her a little space but not too much and to watch her like a hawk. The emotions she was throwing off were a kaleidoscope, and he had the feeling she could be very unpredictable at the moment. And that was never a good thing.

Kristen tossed the beach bag over her shoulder and walked down the crushed shale road leading right up to the dock.

She had a few tricks up her sleeve, too.

While dating a flight instructor she had gotten her pilot's license. So even if she said she could not walk away, she had not promised she would not fly away. She prayed Robert would not have her arrested for stealing his plane. Everything she needed was in her pocket—her passport and billfold. Everything else was replaceable. That included everything except her heart.

~*****~

Slade sensed what she was up to and tore out after her. Radioing the guards to stop her, he was too late as she throttled up just as he reached the beginning of the long pier and boat ramp. He was just behind the two guards.

"Kristen, no!" he yelled. "Stop! It isn't safe!" he shouted, frantically waving his arms above his head and motioning her to return to the dock.

The plane had a gas leak in the main fuel line, and he was waiting on a replacement part, which was due to arrive the day after tomorrow. Until then it was unsafe to fly for several reasons. If she tried this stunt, she would not make it to dry land. She would run out of fuel and crash into the open water. That was only if the plane did not first explode in midair. He ran as fast as he could to the end of the pier to try and reach her. He skidded to a stop just at the end of the dock cursing her for this foolish overreaction.

He watched as she pulled the M7-260 Maule seaplane around for her final throttle up before she would gain enough speed to get lift. There was no other way to communicate with her, so he began to take a leak off the end of the dock, gesturing to the stream and pointing to the plane.

Slade just prayed Kristen understood he was trying to tell her something.

"What the hell is he doing? Taking a leak?" Then she smelled the fuel. "Oh! The plane has a leak!"

She shut the plane down immediately once it sunk in what he was doing. She was almost laughing at the method he had used to communicate with her.

"He is nothing if not resourceful."

She let the plane bob in the water, waiting for him to get there with the boat to tow the plane back to the dock.

"Oh boy, this is not going to be pretty," she said as he got closer to the aircraft.

Slade was furious.

"What the hell do you think you're doing?" he yelled the moment she threw the door open. "Do you realize you could have saved the killer a lot of trouble by doing it yourself? Get out." He gestured for her to take his hand. "Get out!" he growled a second time, concerned that the whole plane would explode. "It's not safe."

She did get out of that plane by jumping into the water and began to swim back to shore causing him to curse in several languages.

What am I going to do with her? he wondered. Her antics and reactions were getting increasingly more self-destructive the longer he had her in captivity.

"Damn it, Kris!" *Shit fire and save the matches,* he thought. "Get back over here and get into this boat. There was a pack of tiger sharks spotted earlier this morning."

She was not getting anywhere near him. She would take her chances with the sharks. At the moment, they looked less a threat than Slade. He was white-hot and angry with her, and it rolled off him in huge waves, nearly sucking the breath from her body. She wasn't afraid of him. He would never do her bodily damage, at least not on purpose. Still, she wanted to give him a chance to decompress.

Slade was thinking this woman was going to make him old before his time. She was stubborn, obstinate, and highly unpredictable. If he got his hands on her, he was going to choke her just to put himself out of the misery of wondering what this woman was going to do next. Kristen was making him crazy, and maybe he deserved some of it but not the heavy dose she was giving him at the moment.

As he tried to get the boat around to get her, she began to laugh as she swam away from him, keeping just out of his reach.

"Get in the boat!" he growled at her.

"I never accept rides from strangers," she said, laughing before going back under.

It just served to make him more upset with her, and seemingly she didn't care. He tossed the life ring to her. "Grab the ring, Kristen, and quit playing around. I'm not in the mood for this."

She went under the water, free diving only to come up yards away from where he had seen her go under the surface. She was getting into shallow water that he could not go with this boat. It was too large a vessel. The coral was dangerously close to the surface here, and any miscalculation could result in ecological damage to the live coral reef or damage to the boat. Both were unacceptable.

"Kris, come back, please. The tides are tricky over there," he yelled, dropping anchor and launching the small rubber raft with the small outboard engine. She went under again and resurfaced closer to the reef edge by a small hilly outcropping at the tip of the island.

He heard the boat before seeing it. In high-speed, Slade saw the boat round that outcropping, heading right for Kristen.

She saw them coming and dove under the water again. However, visibility was superb in the crystal-blue seas of this southern Caribbean island, and it was easy to follow her. Before Slade could reach her, they plucked her up out of the water, dragging her into the boat by her hair. Using the back of her collar, they unceremoniously dumped her into the bottom of that vessel. They were too far for Slade's pistol to be effective, and the M16 was back at the villa.

"Slade! Slade!" she screamed, trying to climb over the side before one of them struck her, knocking her out cold.

Slade roared at the sight of her physical assault as they continued to head out for deeper waters. Slade watched the boat bouncing hard in the waves as it sped away. It had to be beating her to pieces lying unconscious in the bottom of that craft.

These men were not the assassin, but something just as vile. These were real live pirates of the Caribbean. There had been some activity in these waters over the last few months. Human trafficking, theft of property, and crafts sunk and claimed as salvage was increasing. Kidnapping for ransom was also on the rise. If he did not do something to stop them from getting into open waters, then Kris was going to be their next victim. Whatever that something was needed to happen, and it needed to happen fast.

He took the smaller craft back to the plane and hopped back into it, praying all the while the engine would start as he cranked the key. Gaining speed as quickly as possible, he pulled the nose up to increase the lift. He caught up with them in no time. Pulling around, he wanted to try to fire a shot through their outboard motor. It would be the best way to stop them before they got to the larger vessel currently pulling up the anchor out in deeper waters. Kristen was much too close to that engine, and he could not risk shooting her in error.

Instead, on his next pass, he dropped a thirty-pound weight designed to help hold the plane at the docks. It went through the bow of the boat, which immediately began to take in more of the more water each time it dipped into the waves from the front. On a third pass, he fired two consecutive shots into two of the three captors, and he watched as their blood turned the water on the boat a muted pink.

If there weren't sharks around before, there would be soon. Sharks would smell the blood of a fresh kill and follow the scent in earnest.

The little plane was sustaining damage from the small arms fire. He had taken one shot in his leg, and two had gone through the wing. He could see Kristen still lying unconscious in the bottom of that boat. If it sank, she would drown. If it did not sink, then the lone captor could well make it to the larger boat. The mother ship was not yet engaging in the fight but soon would be. He could take that to the bank.

Just about that time, the AK-47 gunfire coming from that larger vessel began whipping all around him. He already had two holes in the left-side wing. He prayed the fuel would last and the line not to ignite.

He saw movement on his last pass. Kris was regaining consciousness. He saw her groping, trying to reach over to pull the weapon from one of the men he shot earlier. With unsteady hands, she pulled the trigger to put a bullet into the back of the one who was still alive and driving the boat at breakneck speed out to open waters. Unfortunately, with all the wave action, she missed, and it didn't kill him, only grazing his shoulder. Slade saw him turn and level his gun at her.

"Oh, no you don't you son of a bitch!" Slade took careful aim and knew he had only one shot, or Kristen would be shark bait. Kristen ducked away from the blood splatter as some of it hit her across the face. The man flew backward onto the throttle, breaking it off in its fully open position. The force of the sudden acceleration and erratic turn back inland pushed her backward nearly out of the back of the boat.

She scrambled back to the controls and tried to steer the speeding craft away from the reef and out to the more open water. However, that was a futile waste of effort. The rudder was twisted and damaged when the unmanned boat ran over a coral head.

"Oh, God!" Slade saw what she was trying to do, and he recognized the erratic movements of the speeding boat. It was a doomed ride.

He had to get her off that craft.

It was going too fast for her to jump. At this speed, she might as well jump onto concrete out of a moving car going sixty. It would kill her or break her in half.

"The engine! Go to the engine!" he yelled inside the cockpit, knowing she could not hear him. He gestured with his hands as he passed overhead circling back and coming in from behind.

She ran back to the back thinking to pull the fuel line off. It was stuck. She needed a knife. She frantically searched the dead bodies, cursing all the while. "You guys are freaking pirates, and none of you are carrying a knife? Shit! Shit! Shit!"

She was running out of time. She looked back over the stern of the boat, meeting Slade's eyes through the windshield of that airplane as he began to gain ground coming from the rear.

He saw her expression of concern and dread begging him to help her. But she hadn't said a word. She didn't have to.

Slade saw the pending catastrophe looming just moments away on the horizon. There were all kinds of small uninhabited islands out here, and the rocks around those islands were deadly. The boat was heading for certain disaster as he made a daring pass over the boat, stretching out the escape ladder.

He had time for one pass and one pass only.

Trying to match the speed of the boat, he watched as she reached for the escape ladder hanging off the left-hand side of the plane.

"Thank you, God!" he said as he felt her weight pull the plane slightly down. He had her. Still there was no time to feel relief.

Plucking her up and veering away just before the boat hit the coral reef and exploded into a fireball, Slade realized his problems were far from over. He had yet bigger troubles to battle. The cockpit was filling with smoke. The craft was on fire, and the engine was sputtering. He had maybe two minutes tops before there would be a point of no return. He grabbed the life jackets from under the front seats. Slipping one on, he clipped the other to his back belt loop.

Slowing the plane and locking the controls, he sent it in a westward heading on a sea-bound path of certain annihilation. Crawling out of the door and onto the pontoons, he lowered himself down to the point where he could hand Kristen the other life vest.

"Put it on!" he yelled above the wind and engine noise while hanging upside down by his knees from the pontoon railings. Once he was sure Kristen was secured, he signaled her to drop. Once she was away, he did a backflip off the plane and into the water. The impact was tremendous even at the reduced height and speed.

Shooting to the surface, he frantically looked around for Kristen and quickly swam the fifteen yards over to her where she bobbed in the water. Her life vest partially detached from the impact that had knocked her out cold. He was lucky. She had landed faceup. Otherwise, he would be attempting in-water resuscitation.

Quickly reaching for her, he fished his arm around and under her arms. Bringing her body on top of his in a survival hold, it also made them look bigger in the water as a further deterrent to any sharks that might come to investigate. His wound was bleeding freely from the shot he took in the leg, and if they were lucky they would not become chum in the water.

First things first, he thought as he popped the shark repellent attached to the lifejacket and watched as it turned a vivid green in the water around them. It might be enough to keep them safe until Chase could get the boat to them. Slade saw him in the distance, closing fast.

Slade revived Kristen as he tread water, holding her securely in his grasp.

"Kris, is anything broken?" he asked, seeing she was conscious.

After spitting the seawater out of her mouth and nose, she assured him she was just dazed. She had a ripping headache, but other than that she was mostly unscathed. Kristen threw her arms around his neck holding on for dear life.

He turned his attention back to the plane, and they watched as it crashed right into the pirates' mothership and exploded upon impact.

He held her close, closing his eyes as a sense of relief completely flooded him. He pulled her head away to look at her face and brushed the wet hair away from her eyes.

"Kris, I…" He began to lower his mouth to hers and at the last minute veered, kissing her cheek, then, settled for a lingering kiss on her forehead. "God, what am I going to do with you?" he asked with his lips still touching her face.

"Apparently, nothing," she pouted, wondering at the fortitude he possessed. He needed to bottle this willpower and sell it to any and all parents of horny, young teenagers. That would stop gratuitous teen sex in its tracks, she mused.

"So, tell me, Slade. When were you going to let me know that you do a little stunt work on the side?" she asked, gaining a healthy respect for this man's abilities.

"So, you admit I'm more than the badge?" It was his feeble attempt at humor.

"Maybe," she said, looking intently into his face as they bobbed in the warm, crystal-blue waters. "What are you, Slade Jericho?" she whispered, realizing her headache and nausea were gone after he kissed her. Just as her arm no longer hurt after he inspected it. She should have bruises and aches yet she felt fine. Where his lips had touched her, she still felt a slight tingle and warmth that triggered a vague memory and a smell of freshly turned earth.

"Your expression says it all. The man that you let me see and the man you are aren't one in the same. You're hiding things from me."

Another truth in her mind? She wasn't entirely sure she wanted to know what those things were, and told him as much.

He brushed her face again and let her go. "Don't ask. Come on; let's get you back to the house."

"You're still the job, Jericho. Guess I figured that one out all by myself. However, I'm no longer sure exactly what the full scope of the job entails. You're no normal homicide cop, Slade. The things I've witnessed over the last few weeks are a testament to the fact that your talents go far beyond solving a murder."

He didn't say anything. It was better not to at this point.

They began to swim back and hadn't gotten a hundred feet when Chase pulled the boat around to retrieve them.

Before getting into the boat, Slade handed Kristen up to Chase. He was not about to leave her in these bloody waters any longer than necessary. He had already been bumped once by a blacktip reef shark.

Seating her in a dry place out of the spray of the water and under cover from scorching rays of the sun, Slade checked her further for any signs of injury that would not have been visible while they were in the water. Once he was satisfied, Slade wrapped a blanket around her before sitting down himself. His leg would have to wait.

"I gather you didn't want dinner guests tonight?" Chase asked Slade as he expertly maneuvered the boat to the docks.

"No. I don't like party crashers." Slade was absolute.

"I'm wondering what I just missed in that exchange. You think that the pirates would have come onto the island later tonight if we hadn't had this encounter?" she asked.

"Yes," Chase said, and then his demeanor changed like quicksilver, and again he turned on the lighter side. "That looked like fun. So, Kris," Chase hollered over his shoulder as he continued to steer the boat, "One to ten and be honest, where would you say that fell on the *holy crap* scale?"

"A big ol'eight," she commented dryly.

"Just an eight?" He quickly pulled up his sunglasses so she could see his eyes and raised a questioning brow.

She nodded. "Yeah, a ten would have been you behind the controls of that plane. I've seen the way you drive." She laughed softly.

"You wound me!" he said, laughing.

"She has a point, Chase," Slade said, agreeing.

As they made their way back to the dock, Kristen acknowledged that if she weren't so totally in love with Slade, Chase might be worth a good chase. That's all a woman would ever get with him. His mamma had named him aptly. She figured one day this man would meet his match, and when that happened, the world might just actually spin backward.

Until then, he would continue to grace the lives of some very lucky ladies. He would completely rock their world, and then leave them feeling like a million bucks. He simply would never commit.

She wondered if he was perhaps taking lessons from Chief Deputy Director Slade Jericho.

~*****~

Chase was looking back at the black smoke billowing from the quickly sinking vessel. If there were survivors, his men would take care of them legally… maybe. It would depend on what they found. From an international law standpoint these assholes were in their waters, and as such they had every right to defend and control the waters around the island within a twelve-mile radius.

"Slade, you do realize that Robert is going to be pissed when he gets wind you crashed and burned his plane. Personally, I'll deny Kris had anything to do with it. It will be your word against ours. Right, kiddo?" Chase teased, yelling above the wave and engine noise of the boat.

Chase understood that men like Robert and himself self-insured for this very reason. They would never find a company to take them on as a client. The line of work calling them was dangerous and deadly, and there wasn't an underwriter in his right mind that would take them on as a client.

They blew things up on a routine basis and never thought anything about it. It simply went with the territory and couldn't be avoided in some instances—like today.

Nevertheless, by his admission, Chase loved his work.

One night while they were all sitting by the pool after dinner, Kristen had asked him why he chose to do what he did for a living.

He hadn't even batted an eye when he told her. "Where else can a guy play with explosives, blow shit up, have super cool toys, shoot totally awesome weapons, and get paid while doing it?"

Seeing that plane go down was nothing new for any of them.

"I'll write Robert a check as soon as I get back to Phoenix," Slade said and turned his attention back to Kristen.

Chase was thinking there might be a mutually beneficial arrangement to be bartered to call it even on the loss of the plane. Chase looked over at Kristen and wondered if there was a way he could use her as part of that bargain.

Chapter 3

Chase arranged to have the golf cart, the only mechanical means of transportation on the island, to be waiting for them when they got back to the pier. Making it back to the house, Slade directed her into the shower to wash off the seawater and to then change into dry clothing.

She had had a shock to her system and was chilled, and he was not entirely sure she didn't have a pretty nasty concussion. He had already done what he could do for her while they were still in the water. There was only so much he could do by external touch alone and, short of her dying, he was never again going to heal her in the ancient ways.

He closed his eyes against the mental picture of her being struck and knocked unconscious. This incident made it twice he had almost lost her. Instead, he focused on the positive things: Kristen alive and safe for the moment.

After her shower, she took her time coming downstairs and into the outdoor kitchen. Slade pulled out a chair and motioned for her to sit down at the table, which had a lovely view into the garden.

"Sit. I need to check you out," he said, watching her closely for any physical signs of instability.

Chase was leaning up against the bar. "Damn, Slade, you need to learn to be more subtle," Chase teased. "I know she is hot and a babe and all, but still…"

"Shut up, Chase."

"Ohhhhh… all right." Chase put up his hands and backed off. "You're certainly in a fine mood."

Slade was in no mood for Chase's crap as he cut his eyes to Kristen, watching carefully for any reaction to Chase's comment. There was none. She was guarding herself, just as he suspected.

Some moments back, he realized that he could no longer hear her thoughts or sense her emotions as he had the previous weeks. His theory was the megadose of adrenaline shot into his system had neutralized any remaining traces of her lingering inside him. He felt relief. Still, having that connection had been comforting, too.

He pulled out one of the chairs and set it in front of her to ensure he had clear access for his examination. He also needed to gain her full and undivided attention. She was looking back at Chase, who was standing just behind her. Chase had one hand on her shoulder and the other on her head gently stroking her hair and giving her head a little shake almost like he would a pet.

"Step back, Chase." Slade's command didn't come out as neutral as he would have liked. The fact Chase was touching her was setting him on edge.

Chase hesitated to snap to attention or follow Slade's command. Looking Slade dead in the eye, Chase purposefully ran his fingers through her hair and then slightly leaned down close enough to smell her.

"Ummm, nice smelling shampoo, kiddo."

"Thanks, I think?" she said.

Slade was not rising to the bait.

Chase never broke eye contact with Slade. It was purely a dominance maneuver on his part. It was a gutsy move; he admitted to himself. Nevertheless, he could hold his own with Slade. Moreover, he needed to keep Slade just a little stirred up where the lovely Doctor Ransom was concerned. If the man got complacent, it would only spell disaster in the future.

However, Chase was not going to push Slade, feeling he had just bumped the line in the sand a little too hard. He removed his hands, putting them up in a show of mock surrender and took a single step back.

Slade never blinked.

By looking at Slade's body language, Kristen was under the impression that he was one breath away from coming across her to get to Chase. She felt Chase take a step back. Once he did Slade finally looked at her but not a second before.

"Look at me," Slade asked her. Gently using his thumb and index finger, he turned her face forward.

"Are you a doctor, too?" Her sarcasm was not lost on either man.

Slade shook his head, having no outward show of going any further with that question.

It was Chase who supplied the answer not letting Slade off the hook.

"Yeah, he's kind of a *doctor*. He actually is an EMT."

Kristen was picking up on all the negative emotion bouncing around the room, and it made her edgy. In her mind, Chase was taking a calculated risk. That comment had probably just earned him a shot that was going to hurt *seriously* the next time he and Slade were in the gym. She had seen Slade fight. The man was powerful.

"Well, aren't you just full of all kind of little surprises?" Kristen said.

Chase jumped in before Slade could say anything, probably sensing his friend was on the ragged edge with her. Come to think of it, Slade was on the ragged edge, period. That was something they all needed to keep in mind.

"She has you there, Slade. Next you will be telling us you're British," Chase joked.

"Only on my mother's side." Slade's dry wit was just what they all needed. It broke the tension and got a small smile from her.

The longer she knew him, the more she was convinced he was hiding something. However, he had the willpower to keep their relationship on a purely platonic level and resist what they felt when they both had the hots for each other. With that being the case, whatever made her think that he would spill his beans on a secret? The man was a freaking vault. She could understand his tactics. That didn't mean she had to like them.

This situation with Slade hurt, and the quicker she could shut herself off, the sooner she would get her world back to level. She pulled deeply into her professional bag of tricks for that technique she used when life had just dished out a little more than she cared to face. She was retreating. It was something everyone had to do at one point or another to live to fight another day.

"Do your fingers like this," he asked.

He demonstrated touching his fingers to his thumb in quick succession. He had her do this on each hand to check her reflexes to ensure she wasn't suffering any loss of motor skill. He nodded his approval.

He looked at her eyes. One was severely bloodshot and probably from the impact of the fall breaking the small vessels in her eye. He took note of the small laceration to the corner where the pirate had backhanded her.

He asked her to close her eyes.

She hesitated.

"Just close your eyes, Kristen. I need to do something with this eyelid," he said, reaching into the first aid kit.

She obeyed, placing her hands on her lap. Slightly slumping forward, she tilted her head back so he could gain access and have better light.

"You have a split on your bottom lip," he said just before he dabbed a small amount of antibiotic ointment on the tip of his finger. He touched her lips, and then her eyelid with the pad of his fingertip.

She felt the warmth. Suddenly, in her mind, she was naked and lying on soft earth. Was that Chase she remembered? And she remembered Slade telling her he was sorry.

Sorry for what, she wondered.

She remembered the smell of grass, water, and something more subtle, almost like musk. Involuntarily, she put her fingers to her lips remembering the warm lingering kiss as Chase's face shimmered and changed. It was Slade, yet she couldn't see him clearly. It was like looking at him through a fog and bubbled glass.

Chase and Slade looked at each other, realizing she was having a flashback. They both felt it, too. It was a strong and powerful pull, reaching deep into their minds for the most impressionable memories. The room filled with the fragrance of a field of wildflowers and freshly mown hay. Chase remembered the day his father had let him drive the tractor for the first time back on the family farm. It was a rite of passage to manhood for the McKinnon boys. It was a memory he had forgotten but was glad it had resurfaced. The breezes blowing in from the ocean cleaned the room of the fresh, clean country smells, and replaced those with the subtle yet heady smell of Kristen's perfume. Slade was remembering how she had smelled and the passion he felt when he slammed that cottage door the night of Chase's party. His emotions were a rollercoaster that night. Things were no different today. The men waited in silence for her to release the room and slowly she opened her eyes.

"What the hell just happened?" she asked and noticed Chase and Slade both shook their head at each other.

"I'm not going to get anything from either of you. Am I?"

"Nothing happened, kiddo." Chase recovered first but didn't have a good answer.

Slade continued to dab at her eyelid. "It is just an aftereffect of the concussion. You may have an episode or two over the next couple of days. Just ignore them as the brain's way of trying to reconnect with reality."

Chase gave Slade a thumbs-up for thinking fast on his feet.

Then Slade held his index finger up in front of her face. "Now, follow my finger." She looked left, following his index finger, and as it came back to center, she took her focus off his finger and looked at him, focusing intently on his face.

"I want to go home," she begged, softly digging her fingers into the sleeve of the lightweight cotton shirt he had put on after getting back to the villa. "I appreciate what you and Chase are doing. Really, I do, but I've got to go home."

"It's too soon." Slade shook his head. Kristen's withdrawal was harder for Slade to swallow than he ever anticipated. It pulled at his gut, wrenching painfully at his heart. When she had walked down to the pier, and he realized she was trying to walk away, he felt his world stop for that brief moment. Her walking away or flying away was inevitable. However, he was not ready yet to let her go.

"No, it's not. I apologize for crowding you. I know you don't want me, Slade, not like I want you. I accept that. However, my patients need me even if you don't."

He momentarily closed his eyes and dropped his chin to his chest before looking back at her.

I need you; he yelled inside his head. He just didn't dare say it and get her hopes up of there ever being anything more between them.

Slade could easily see the change in her. She had given up on him. He wanted to argue. He wanted to tell her she was wrong, that he did need her, and that she needed to let him continue to protect her here in this paradise far, far away from the real world. He wanted her to stay here where he could have her to himself and to be with her in the only way that was ever possible.

However, there was something in her voice and eyes that said he was not winning this one. He was finally getting what he deserved. So, picking his battles, he decided this was one he would not wage, not today.

He cupped her face, rubbing his thumb across her cheek. "All right," he relented, slowly nodding his consent, "if that's what you truly want, then we'll leave just as soon as we can get a craft here."

"It doesn't matter what I want, Slade. You've shown me that much already. I never asked for this," she said, waving her hand around at the five grown men, the butler, and a chef at her beck and call.

Slade understood that Kristen hadn't asked him to whisk her away. She had not asked her heart to betray her. Nonetheless, she had all those things. The one thing Kris didn't have and all she ever wanted was to find her sister's murderer.

It tore at him to know that once she was back in Dallas and back in her home, on her turf, his place would no longer be at her side.

He sensed the wall go up, felt her withdraw, and his guts wrenched painfully. This situation was partly his fault, and he would own it where he needed to.

"If we had met under different circumstances… I could have…" he said and let the sentence trail off.

She nodded, the tears swimming in her golden-green eyes. "I know."

Chase watched as Kristen dropped her forehead back on Slade's shoulder for a brief moment as he cupped the back of her head, gently stroking her hair. Slade looked at him and softly tilted his head to the side indicating he needed a few moments alone with her.

Chase nodded his understanding as he walked out of the room, taking the rest of the men with him. This scene was not one he wanted or needed to see. It was personal and private, and it was between Slade and Kristen. Chase's first thought was *Ouch; that's going to hurt.* His second was something along the lines of *Too bad there's nothing to stop this train wreck.*

She was saying goodbye. That left Chase feeling like he was the odd man out. However, it was painful for all three of them. He cared about both of them, and his friend was going to have to let her go. It was the only way Slade would ever have her in a way that did not make him feel guilty.

In the meantime, it was going to hurt like hell for Slade. It would hurt Kristen too, for that matter, until Slade figured it all out.

Chase did not envy the man. That kind of pain is what love will get you.

The poor bastard, better him than me, he thought. He just hated that Kristen was being dragged through hell right along with Slade.

~*****~

Hurt like hell—that didn't even come close to describing what Slade was feeling. He continued to sit there after she got up from the chair. He reached out and grabbed her hand as she walked past, and the only thing he could do was to kiss it and let her go. The only acknowledgment from her that she even remotely felt his pain was the hand she gently dragged across his shoulder as she walked past him and away.

Slade wasted no time going in search of the one person he felt Kristen would let near her at the moment. He found Chase out on the front steps of the villa smoking a fine Cuban cigar and drinking a glass of bourbon straight up.

"Go to her," Slade commanded on his way past, heading for the gym complex. He needed to beat the shit out of something.

Chase slammed back the contents of his glass in a single swallow, took one more drag on the cigar, tossed it to the ground, and nodded once as he ground it with his deck shoe.

As Slade beat that kick bag completely into pieces, Kristen cried, and it was Chase who was drying her tears.

Chapter 4

Dallas, Texas

Just outside the city of Dallas, Slade stood on the stoop of Kristen's home waiting for her to invite him in. He was not going to make the assumption he was welcome. It was not that she was cold to him.

She wasn't. It was the opposite.

She was cordial and accommodating, almost passive in her dealing with the circumstances now that he had agreed to take her home. He had agreed under one condition; he would let her board that flight back to Dallas only if he could supply a doubled-up security team.

Kristen's behavior somewhat reminded him of the first morning after they found Kari dead. Just as she was mourning the loss of her sister, she was mourning the loss of their doomed relationship. Maybe he was, too.

No, she hadn't been cold. It was just the fact she had begun to squeeze him out over the last three days since she asked him to take her home. She immediately stopped her evening ritual of coming to his room even though he kept the door open instead of locked. He had wanted her to feel she was still welcome. Their conversations continued to be affable but no longer of a personal nature. She didn't allow him to touch her at all, in any way or anytime.

He tried to get her alone to talk. Somehow, she always managed to have Liz, Zane, or Chase close at hand, mostly Chase. The laughter she and Chase shared made Slade even crazier than the night at the party when all the men were hovering around her like bees to nectar. She was developing a deeper friendship with Chase. Chase wasn't doing anything to stop it.

Chase and Slade didn't discuss the kiss the night he saved her, simply to keep the peace. Slade had certainly felt the lust, not love, in that second kiss Chase had taken purely for himself. Lust was still a driving emotion, but one Kristen didn't need. As a result, Slade was watching his friend closely ever since they had begun to make preparations to leave the island.

It was making Slade insane. He was watching for any actions that even remotely came close to the line that Slade had set in his mind. He had no right to tell Chase to back off because there wasn't anything Chase was overtly doing. Chase was just being Chase and a good friend who loved and understood women beyond all logic.

Besides, Chase had said that he would have to be prepared to defend his right to her unless he fully claimed her. Slade didn't want Chase as a competitor, certainly not over a woman. However, much more and it would come down to exactly that. Still, Chase was the only man Slade trusted with her. Even that trust was wearing extremely thin.

That edginess had resulted in a heated argument between the men about her protection once she got back to Dallas. Slade felt Chase needed to stay on the sidelines, feeling even Chase was too close to her to be of any real security. Chase told him to go to hell and that he would leave if Kristen wanted him to leave her alone, and not until then.

Chase had argued a point and argued that point well; Kristen needed someone around her that would be there as a friend and not as a hired gun.

Slade finally agreed, with the express promise that Chase would never, ever spend the night. The warning Slade delivered was not even thinly veiled. If Chase took advantage of Kristen and touched her, Slade would come after him with a vengeance.

"Come on in. Make yourself at home," Kristen offered, looking back over her shoulder as she dropped her bag inside the front door. She waved Slade inside just as she leaned down and picked up her dog, a mangy, little mongrel that was most happy to see her.

"Hey, Doody. Did you miss me, girl?" she asked, playing with the Maltese-poodle mix that was nothing more than a ball of fluff and a long, wet tongue.

The Rottweiler named Tank was another story, entirely. Lucky for Slade, the animal was highly trained in obedience and followed Kristen's every command.

In the dog's mind just because his mistress had told him to sit and stay, it didn't mean he had to sit and stay there quietly. The deep growl said it all. Slade felt better knowing she had Tank in the house with her.

Slade almost hoped Tank would bite Chase on the ass. Somehow, he needed to get past that attitude. He also needed to get past this jaws-on-paws without that very thing happening to him.

"Hey, boy, I'm one of the good guys," he coaxed.

Kristen snapped her fingers twice, and the dog looked at her. "Tank, you show-off! Stop that and say hello." She pointed her finger toward Slade.

Instantly, the dog began to wag his nubby tail and prance around Slade's legs for attention. Slade held his fist out for Tank to smell and knew he was home free when the dog licked his hand.

Kristen handed him a wet hand wipe from the tub she had sitting handy on the entry hall table. Apparently, dog slobber in her house was nothing new.

Slade dropped his bag just inside the door of the two-story English Tudor nestled in an older and very sedate part of town. He wouldn't be staying long in the house, just long enough to get her settled. His plan was to check out the house, ensuring all was secure, and then sit tight to wait for the arrival of her Dallas security team.

In the meantime, Liz and Zane Colvin, Randy's replacement, had met them at the airport to guarantee Kristen had ample coverage for the transport from there to here.

The six new and freshly briefed operatives were set to relieve Liz and Zane just as soon as they could get there from the briefing in downtown Dallas at the central offices of McKinnon-Bride Personal Security.

Chase was noticeably absent, and no one had seen him since they left the airport. He had gotten off the plane, gave Kristen a one-armed hug and a kiss on her head while shaking Slade's hand at the same time. Then Chase got in his car without much more than a "see ya," leaving them in the hands of his younger brother, Mason, who drove them to the house under heavy guard.

Slade was impressed with the standard of this company. Even if there had been a slip-up or two, the overall professionalism was outstanding. This operation was a well-oiled machine, and if he had to leave her in someone else's hands, these were hands he trusted.

Whoever killed Kari had sufficient time to figure out where Kristen lived, and it wouldn't be long before they figured out she was back in town.

The shapeshifter already knew where she lived. That was a topic he and Chase had discussed at great length.

Before they left the Caribbean, Chase had assured Slade that he had a trained scent dog on the way to Kristen's house, who would check out the grounds, and he would keep the dog around for as long as necessary. It was the only way Slade would allow her to stay on the premises.

Regardless of the fact that her protection was now up to nearly five grand a day with the addition of the dog and the extra guards, he didn't care how much it cost. It was only money, and he could afford it as long as it didn't drag on indefinitely.

The animal was worth every penny being highly trained to smell and track various otherworldly creatures such as a shifter or vampire. It could pull the scent from even the faintest traces. If the shifter had already been there, they would know immediately. Slade appreciated the offer of the animal and thought it was smart, but he had to wonder if Chase was bringing in dogs to keep him at bay. As a symbiotic healer, he was technically a shapeshifter. If the dogs were there, the dog would sniff Slade out, too. Hence, he could be nowhere around if the dog was present. Chase told him that wouldn't be the case if he simply came clean with Kristen about his genetic makeup. Eventually, he would have to come clean if they ever got to the point of dating. That was not today.

Once the new security team settled in, and he was satisfied with their performance, he would leave Dallas by the end of the week unless she asked him to stay. He didn't want to leave her. Nevertheless, even if he stayed it would only forestall the inevitable.

They hadn't spoken about it because there was nothing to talk about in Kristen's mind. The time had come, and as much as he might want to stay, it just wasn't in the cards.

He had less than ten days to report to Broken Arrow. There was no forestalling, as he had already gotten another week reprieve. He had pushed it as far as he could. Nonetheless, he would stay in a heartbeat if she asked him, and he had told her so on several occasions. However, on that count, he wasn't holding his breath.

She understood his dilemma, already stating she would not have him sacrifice his work for her when the McKinnon team was the best money could buy.

The team had her covered, and there was no need for him to stay except for purely personal reasons.

Slade understood that she wouldn't ask him to remain beyond the end of the week. In her mind, she had already said goodbye before they ever left the island.

He still had a few days left in Dallas, and he would spend as much time with her as she would allow. Then they would just see once he settled in. He would still have to be in contact with her if for no other reason than her sister's murder was still hanging out there unresolved. If he could leave the lines of communication open then eventually things might come together for them as long as the Council of Violations of the Vampire Nation never discovered what he had done with her. That was hanging like an ax over his head. He felt he had found a loophole in the law but hoped he never had to try it as a defense. It was weak at best.

"The house is secure," Liz said as she came back to the front door to announce that they could continue further into the house.

With the area safe, Slade needed to contact Detective Lacy to see what was going on with the case and if Detective Green had ever surfaced.

"Can I use your phone?" Slade asked. "I need a secure landline."

She nodded before leading him into her office.

"Make yourself at home. The phone is there on my desk," she offered before closing the sliding pocket doors to her study.

~*****~

Slade looked around one of Kristen's most quiet spaces. Signs of her were everywhere. The stack of well-read magazines on the small antique coffee table, the empty coffee mug with the light pink lipstick on the rim sitting by her computer monitor, and the book placed open and facedown on the end table to mark her place were all signs she used this room routinely.

He didn't sit in her chair. He wasn't going to make himself that much at home.

Instead, he turned the phone around on her desk and used the guest chair.

"Lacy? It's Slade. What did you find out?" he asked once he got the detective on the phone.

What Slade found out was that The Phoenix Museum of Modern and Geological Arts was looted in a robbery. The thieves took millions of dollars' worth of rare gems and several pieces of art in that heist.

Lacy was flipping through his notes. Slade could hear the rustle of the papers. "It's looking like the night guards were overpowered by a bogus cleaning crew."

"Alive or dead?" Slade asked, wondering if they had been lucky enough to be tied up and left in a storeroom.

"Dead." Lacy's answer was brief.

"How many?" Slade asked, pinching the bridge of his nose. He hadn't gotten much sleep the night before, and it was beginning to grind on him. He wasn't getting any younger and the long days were beginning to tell. With Kristen backing away, he wasn't standing on smooth emotional ground either, only making it worse.

"Five total—two women and three men. The murders were quick and professional."

"I'm guessing the kind of money we're talking about for this heist it was worth ensuring no witnesses were left.

What else can you tell me?" Slade asked, reaching for the photo frame on her desk. He turned it around. It was a young version of Kristen sitting on a street curb with a little blond-haired, blue-eyed boy between her knobby knees. She was hugging him tightly and grinning like a Cheshire cat, eyes full of mischief. He smiled. The young boy had to be Stephen, her brother. The coloring difference was stark, yet they looked amazingly alike as far as the facial features were concerned. On impulse, he made a photocopy of the picture before placing it back on her desk.

"I'm checking the ballistics report to see if any of the bullets came from the same gun used at Chase's party."

Slade watched out the window as two new guards began to make the rounds and swallowed hard when he saw Chase and not one but two dogs pile out of the back of a dark-blue van.

Obviously, Chase is a firm believer in redundancy, Slade thought.

"Well, just great," Slade murmured under his breath as he watched Chase take one dog by his lead and the second dog disappear around the corner led by another guard.

"What?" Lacy asked. "Something just grabbed your attention."

65

"Nothing, except that things have just gone to the dogs," he said dryly and let the curtain fall back into place.

Tank was most unhappy at this intrusion into his domain and was very vocal about it. Slade could relate as he watched Chase maneuver the dog through the front lawn in a zigzag pattern, looking for even the slightest trace.

Slade, needing to wrap this conversation up quickly, found out that all surveillance tapes were erased or destroyed except a small piece. Lacy didn't know what was on it in the way of evidence if anything at all. The partial clip was being sent to the forensic lab to see what they could pull off of it.

The vandals systematically crashed display cases all over the museum. Coincidentally, they had known which of the cases the alarm system wasn't attached.

Not what you would call classified information, Slade thought. Lacy confirmed.

"That information would have been relatively easy to collect just by going to the museum. On the surface, you might think that it doesn't tell us much about the perpetrators. Once you think about it, in actuality it does. They were smart enough to choose those cases that wouldn't trip the alarm, so they had time to make a clean getaway without the attention of the alarms."

"Right. I follow," Slade agreed. "And, they had to have some activity that justify the deaths of the guards without triggering a comprehensive inventory of the museum."

They planned the heist well. The thieves had taken smaller items of value. The items were important but not rare and certainly not the kind of items that sell well on the black market. Slade figured these were simply a way of distracting the investigators away from the real items lifted during the heist.

The permits Kari had uncovered were making more sense to him, and the chief had turned the evidence of the permitting errors and possible bribes resulting from them over to the FBI.

"Why the FBI?" Slade wondered.

Lacy filled him in. "If there's an upside, it's the fact the thief made a tactical error. One of the pieces of artwork was on loan from the Smithsonian."

The art is the property of the US government and given to the American people by a patron of the arts in 1818. That meant that this murder and robbery investigation had the full backing of the federal government with resources dwarfing those of the Phoenix police homicide and burglary units.

Slade was curious. "The phony cleaning crew, even if inside the museum, wouldn't be allowed to pass inside a certain perimeter of the artwork. Otherwise, the pressure sensors would trip the alarm. So, how did they get by with it?"

"The thieves came in from under the floor, lifting the artwork off the walls without ever tripping a sensor," Lacy said.

He almost sounded impressed to Slade's trained ear.

By coming up through the basement ceiling, the thief had a one-foot space that was unsecured between the sensor pad and the baseboard. That small space kept rodents running along the perimeter from falsely setting off the alarm systems. To hedge their bets, somehow the thief had triggered several false-alarm calls in the two weeks preceding the robbery. That prompted a systems engineer making a visit to the museum. That analysis resulted in a recommendation to adjust the sensitivity of the sensors for a greater tolerance range. It played right into the thief's plan. Once the engineer increased sensitivity levels of the sensor pads to a higher tolerance, the thief had simply cut a rectangular hole in the floor and dropped the paintings through using a hooking device that they left behind. They hung the forgeries back in their original's place and replaced the carpet back over the hole once done.

"The only reason they even knew the art was gone was one of the frames didn't have a dent in it where it was supposed to have one. Out of the mouths of babes," Lacy expounded.

Two days after the museum opened back up to the public, a school kid had pointed out the fact the dent wasn't there. The kid said he remembered it from the last field trip because it looked like the shape of a bear, and it was the only thing interesting about the painting. There was no bear-shaped dent on that frame, resulting in the launching of the investigation.

The fakes were very well done, all the work of master forgers, and there were only two individuals in the world that good.

"Corsazie or Lentil?" Slade asked, knowing that these two artists were the best from a case he worked several years back. However, according to Lacy, Harvey Lentil was in prison doing twenty consecutive ten-year terms for counterfeiting. That potentially ruled him out in Slade's mind, nevertheless, not entirely. Many a criminal continued to lead a life of crime while still behind bars.

"If it was Corsazie, we'll never know." Lacy let Slade know that the artist was recently found dead of a heroin overdose in a back room in Bangkok. He was not going to sing except to the angel Gabriel.

His death was too coincidental in Slade's mind. Getting the Bangkok police to investigate in detail was looking like a long shot. Opium den deaths were a dime a dozen in a city where you could buy any decadence a deviant could conjure in his or her mind. What was a dead Italian artist to them?

"So, how did they get out with the goods?" Slade asked, hearing the smaller of the two scent dogs barking by the front door.

Oh, man, I am busted, he thought, remembering his suitcase by the front door. Then the dog went quiet again.

"They tunneled out," Lacy answered, bringing Slade back to the conversation.

The tunnel from the excavation was a perfect escape route. It bumped out in a small closed-off, seldom-used storeroom in the basement of the museum. Several businesses were breached to toss the investigators off the scent, and to shift blame to all as potential suspects because they all had access. And it would have worked, except Kari had uncovered the bogus permits.

The only external exit outside of the tunnel ended at a manhole in a blind alley in the restaurant district almost a block away from the museum. No one would have given a second thought to a delivery van making a pickup in an alley.

Apparently, that was the case as there wasn't a single person the detectives could rustle up who remembered anything unusual. All video leads gathered from the surrounding area checked out to be legitimate deliveries. And, as luck would have it, there weren't any video sources available for that particular alleyway.

"And what about the Shake diamond?" Slade needed to stop asking questions and get the hell off the phone, but he needed answers, and the only way to get them was to ask the questions while he had a secure line.

"Gone and they don't know when or how, either."

"The Shake diamond wasn't thought to have been taken in the heist? I would have thought that security would have jumped on that piece first."

"No alarms tripped," was Lacy's response.

There were silent alarms that should have been activated no matter how much the system had been dialed down. The alarm company saw no break in the system, no glitch, and no interruption of power surrounding the diamond.

"However, once they got the gemologist in to have a look, then she found it was a fake as well. It hit the fan, too, trust me. Tracing the source of a fake gem isn't as easy as the forgery of a masterpiece." Lacy had already looked into the possibility of the individuals known to forge large and famous gemstones. With the fall of the USSR, many of the Russian royal jewels had come up missing, and top of the list of usual suspects was a woman by the name of Sophia Romeo. In her heyday, she was a young, beautiful, and a highly intelligent woman. Too bad she was a thief and had gone to ground some years ago. At this point, the woman could be anywhere.

Slade was still puzzling that out. "It's tough but not impossible to forge and track a gemstone. I'll see if Chase is interested in running this one down. If it involves an attractive piece of tail, I'm sure he'd jump on it."

In Slade's mind, all this meant was that the fake had been on display the whole time with the real heist having taken place long before now or the day the diamond first came out of the vault.

Lacy was one step ahead of Slade on this one.

"I'm trying to ferret out who had access to the diamond from the time the vault was open until the time security placed it under that bulletproof glass. Fortunately, the FBI looks like they're taking this one very seriously, Slade."

"Good," Slade said nervously, hearing the dog coming ever closer, urged on by Chase's commands. Slade wondered if Lacy could sense his anxiety.

"I think I'll be able to get back on the murders of Kari and the senator. I'm with you on this one, Slade. The two murders are somehow intertwined. We just have to find that common connection."

"Try Thomas Levine and a warehouse he owns on the south side of town." That was all Slade could say as he had nothing else much to go on except a few vague notes and an address.

"Senator Levine?" Lacy asked in surprise.

Thomas Levine was now Senator Levine, having won by a landslide in the special election, and if Slade's sources were correct, then Levine was on his way to Washington. He was already presenting a bill to the House and Senate to have stronger control over the borders. Slade knew it was a crock of bullshit and a ploy to gain lobbying dollars. With

Levine's sights on the Oval Office, even if he was rich, he still needed the campaign dollars to get there.

"Yeah, that Levine. One and the same. Listen, I've got to go. I hear the dogs barking."

Slade hung up with Detective Lacy feeling that they were still no closer to solving the murder of the senator or Kari than the day he first walked into this mess. It was looking like he was leaving the department with not just one but two open cases and letting Kristen down in the process.

As if his thoughts conjured her, Kristen opened the sliding door to her office. He was standing there staring out the window with his arms crossed over his chest, deeply lost in thought.

"Slade? I'm sorry to disturb you. Whatever it was that you found out from Detective Lacy was not what you wanted to hear. Was it?"

He turned from the window at the sound of his name.

Kristen was standing in the office doorway holding out a package for him. How had he ever felt his life was complete before she entered his world? He saw now just how hollow it truly was without her.

"Kristen, close the door and come in here a moment."

"What is it?" She slid that door closed in front of Tank, who was scratching the door to get to her.

Slade waited for her to come and stand next to him.

"Slade, what's eating at you?"

Slade was not surprised by the question. She was a therapist and saw right through him even on a good day of him hiding things from her. He wasn't hiding anything today.

He got straight to the point. "Would you have done things differently had I simply been a beat cop, or just a detective, and not in line for promotion?"

She shook her head, not as an answer. She shook her head because it was dirty pool. "That's not a fair question, Slade. It's hypothetical and immaterial."

"I wouldn't ask if I didn't have a reason."

"All right," she said, hesitating over her answer. "I think the fairer question in this particular instance would be this: would *you* have done things differently?"

He hesitated. "Honestly, I just don't know, baby. Some things weigh in here that have nothing to do with the chief's job. If I've seemed, well, unresponsive, I've had my reasons, and they aren't because I don't have positive feelings for you."

He was certain that Kristen had already figured that out. She just had no idea what those other things were that had kept him from crossing the line with her.

"You don't have to try and salve over my feelings, Slade. I get it."

"No, I don't think you do. You couldn't possibly get it. I don't get it, even having all the pieces." He cupped her face, gently rubbing the pad of his thumb over her cheek. It was the first time she had allowed him to touch her since the pirates almost abducted her from the island.

"Oh, God," she said looking into his eyes, "here it comes, the 'it's me, not you' speech."

She automatically took a step back and crossed her arms. She did it to protect herself.

He nodded at her acute perception. "It *is* my fault, and I just can't leave here letting you think that what I feel for you is the reason that I've shown so much restraint. In reality, it is, but not why you might think." He sighed in exasperation. Never in his life had he felt so backed against a wall.

"Slade, listen, sometimes things are just not meant to go the distance. In our case, well," she shrugged and stepped away, "I guess you can safely say we never got out of the gate." She handed the package out to him and continued, "Here, this came here for you."

"Thank you," he said as he reached for the package. " I appreciate you letting me have my mail sent here until I can find a place in Broken Arrow."

"Certainly. It is no problem," she said.

He looked at the package. It had a Phoenix postmark clearly on the front but showed no return address. He was instantly suspicious. Slade had Chase *call in a favor* of one of his buddies on the police force requesting that someone from the bomb squad come over. Neither man was going to let his guard down at this juncture.

What they found inside that package wasn't a bomb. Nonetheless, it blew up in Slade's face all the same.

~*****~

"Detective, I think you need to take a look at this." The young officer from the bomb squad waved Slade over.

"Do you have any idea what this is about?" the commander in charge asked after pulling off his flak jacket and pushing up his helmet shield.

The dogs were going crazy, barking and pulling at the lead hard enough that Chase and the other handler were

77

having problems controlling the animals. He and Chase were certain that package had enemy DNA all over it. They were just not certain who the enemy was… yet. If Chase could get the scent, it might prove useful down the line.

Slade watched as Kristen looked down at the drugs, one-hundred dollar bills neatly shrink-wrapped in bundles, and the note stating this was his share of the take from the sale of the stolen museum items, less the cost of the forgeries.

Kristen also saw the missing key to Kari's house. It was attached on one of those types of rings that are joined at the middle with a separate ring at each end. You could pull them apart and separate the rings if necessary.

"This one is the other half of the one I saw sitting on your dresser the first night I was in your house."

There was a note attached to the key ring. Kristen read it aloud. "This came in handy in killing the Ransom girl, good work."

All of it just sealed the deal to make him look guilty of a crime he did not commit.

Kristen turned to the senior officer in charge. "Is there anything else you need from me?"

Slade watched as the color drained from her face. She somewhat swayed as if the world was slightly spinning.

"No, ma'am. Detective Jericho and I will get this cleared up down at the station. There has to be a logical explanation."

She turned without a word.

"Kristen?" Slade watched her walk up the steps to her front door. "Kris, wait." He hurried to catch up.

He put the toe of his boot at the base of the door to keep her from closing it. "I'm being set up. Let me in so we can talk this out. I swear I don't know what this is about, but I will get to the bottom of it. You have to believe me." The tears glistening in her eyes ripped a new hole in him. "Baby, you have to know who I am by now." She just looked at him with an expression of hurt and confusion etched deeply on her features. "Kristen, for God's sake, please, just follow your heart. You know me."

"Do I? Or do I just know the man you want the rest of the world to see?"

He watched as her eyes darted to his gun. She had seen him in action over the last several weeks. She had witnessed him in a different setting and a different world than most would ever see him, and he kept those two lives separate on purpose. He had lived a double life for years and few ever really knew him. He had walked that tightwire since college, managing to keep his two distinct lives from blending, until now.

He answered her unspoken question.

He kept his voice low. "Yes, Kris. When the act is justified, I am capable of killing. You know that and have even witnessed it, and I won't deny it. It's part of the job. Without batting an eye, I would kill anyone daring to lay a hand on you to harm you, but I could never have killed her. She was an innocent."

He waited for her to say something. She closed her eyes tightly, and he saw one of those tears escape, running down her cheek.

"Kristen? Please, talk to me."

"All I know anymore, Slade, is that my sister is dead, and her killer could be almost anyone," she said, closing the door.

Those tears swimming in her eyes were hard for him to take but were nothing next to her broken trust.

Maybe he deserved it.

Maybe this was his punishment for not fully appreciating the gift fate had given him. He stood there looking at that closed door and continued to knock.

"She's an intelligent woman, Slade," Chase spoke softly from behind him. "She will sort it all out in her own time. Let her go for now."

Slade turned to look into jade-green eyes, which were older and harder than Slade had ever seen. "Hmm, easier said than done. I'm in love with her, Chase."

Chase shrugged as if that were a foregone conclusion. "Of those who understand and know her, who wouldn't be just a little in love with her? She will eventually come around. In the meantime, lend that which you cherish most unto my safekeeping. I will shelter it as if it were my own."

Chase's unexpected statement took Slade by surprise.

"But she isn't yours," Slade growled, wondering if he was making a mistake leaving Kris in Chase's tender care.

Chase snapped back. "And I'm thinking she doesn't belong to you either, Slade. And, from what I saw on that island, it wasn't from lack of her being willing either. I wonder if she's tired of the Arizona freeze and might be interested in a little Texas heat."

Slade grabbed Chase by the shirt and pulled him closer, their noses all but touching. "She had better be in the same shape as how I have left her when I return, you understand me, McKinnon? She isn't a piece of property to own or a piece of ass to be sampled." Slade let him go, pushing back just enough to punctuate his point.

Slade had just about had enough. Chase was again walking a fine line with him, and he wondered at what point Chase would cross that line.

"Oh, I think you're wrong about that piece of ass part, but I'll try to keep that in mind."

"Good idea." Slade was not convinced. But he had to trust Chase. Could he?

Chase liked Kristen and found her an appetizing morsel. By this time in a relationship and under normal circumstances, if she were receptive, Chase would have already pounced, figuring Slade had time to do the deed if he was going to do it. However, for whatever reason he wasn't inclined to pursue her as a "piece of ass." He liked her more than a sister but less than a girlfriend and felt protective toward her. That being the case, he wasn't going to infringe where he shouldn't, and he had found he was doing that more and more of late and not just with women.

Scary, he thought, because he could see the benefits of not pursuing a woman for a change.

Chase's priority, second to keeping her alive, was keeping her untouched. He would make sure that no one else had access to her until Slade could pull his head out of his ass and finally see what he needed to do about the lovely Doctor Ransom.

He wasn't going to tell Slade that he was not a player in this game, at least not for the moment. Someone needed to keep Slade on the edge. Eventually, they all would reach a point of no return. If Slade did not claim her, Chase felt obligated to do so, just to ensure she had a man who understood her and would treat her with respect. The wrong man could make her life a living nightmare, forcing her to bend to his perverted wishes. Chase would marry her before letting that happen, even if he felt Slade was the better match.

"You do that," Slade said, looking down at the dog, who was obediently sitting at Chase's heel, panting in a steady rhythm. The animal was completely calm and oblivious to Slade's presence.

"By the way," Chase said, passing the two shirts that he had lifted from their suitcases over to Slade, "here are your and Kristen's shirts back." By having the two scents together, the dog would associate Slade's scent was friendly even if he was the same classification as a shapeshifter.

"I owe you one," Slade begrudgingly admitted.

"Damn right, you owe me, Jericho. I'm covering your ass with the dogs for her sake, not yours, and, just for the record, I think you're a dumb ass for not pushing your hand with her while you still have that option." Chase cocked his head at him. "I would sure hate to see you wake up one morning and realize you waited for one too many sunrises to stake that claim." With that, he turned. "Come on, boy," Chase said to the dog, never looking back at Slade.

Chapter 5

Phoenix, Arizona
11:00 p.m.

Kristen worked well into the evening and was sitting at the desk in her hotel room getting less than nothing accomplished. Rubbing her hands over her tired face, she then picked up her phone for the third time that evening and finally mustered up the nerve to call.

Her hands were sweaty as she heard the ring and took in a breath when she heard his voice thinking it was Slade on the other end. She let that breath out in disappointment once she realized it was his voice mail, yet again.

"Leave a message after the tone. I'll call you as soon as I can."

"Hey… It's me." Then, taking a deep breath for courage, she continued. "Listen…" she slightly paused, "I've been thinking about something, and it may be nothing at all, but still, if you can call me, I would appreciate it. So, call me if you get this message." She hesitated again. "Slade, I wanted to say that, maybe… well, if things were different…" her voice trailed off and dropped almost to a whisper. "I'll talk to you soon."

Kristen softly placed her cell phone back on the charger resting on the nightstand. She stood up and stretched, deciding to call it a night, and headed for the shower.

~*****~

On the other side of town, Slade got out of the shower and was dressing to meet Lacy at the station house for an update. He might be officially off the force, but he still needed to find Kari's killer. He had promised Kristen he would find Kari's killer, and he was going to keep that promise.

Getting ready to walk out the back door, he picked up his keys and phone and noticed the voice mail indicator on the screen. It was a missed call from Kristen.

"Damn it," he cursed under his breath. He had been trying to reach her for almost a week.

Chase had briefed him and told him that after he had left Dallas, Kristen had locked herself in her home office and had barely come out for the first seventy-two hours except to teach her classes at the university that had started just after they returned to Dallas. She had seen an attorney, was seeing patients almost around-the-clock in her study and was screaming at her editor about some mix-up on a deadline with her publisher.

Now, according to his assistant chief, for whatever reason that escaped him, Kristen was back in Phoenix. Chase wasn't with her, which didn't bode well, not in Slade's mind. She had given Chase the slip in Dallas one evening just after he left to go home. Now, Slade was kicking himself for not allowing Chase to sleep over at her house. So, here she was in Phoenix, poking around where she shouldn't be all because he was jealous of a man who might, in reality, be good for her.

Slade didn't feel she was intentionally avoiding his calls. She would be more likely to pick up the phone and tell him to go straight to hell. So, since she called that could mean a couple of things. She was softening, or she had some evidence to share. From her message, it sounded like the latter over the former although there was a glimmer of hope even then. He would still take it, however, small that glimmer might be.

He called her back immediately.

"Leave me a message. If this is a medical emergency, please call 911 for emergency assistance."

"Hey, Kris, sorry I missed you. I was in the shower. I'm meeting Lacy for a briefing on the case here in a little

87

while. I know it's late, but let me take you for a late dinner after the meeting. I know you're in town, and I would love to see you. Call me. It doesn't matter what time."

Slade hung up the phone and heard the front doorbell.

He looked out to see Detectives Lacy and Phillips as well as Chief Holiday standing on his porch.

"Hey, guys, what's up? Come to tell me how much you're going to miss me?" he asked after he opened the door. He was wondering if they were there to say their final goodbyes. They had worked together for a lot of years, and this was his final night here. He was putting the final touches on the house before turning it over to the new owners and leaving Phoenix for good the next afternoon.

"Slade, we came to warn you. An officer from internal affairs is on the way to pick you up."

"What the hell for?" Slade couldn't imagine what the hell was going on.

There was absolutely no reason for internal affairs to be interested in him. He had been a good boy and kept his hands to himself.

"For the murders of the museum guards, possession of stolen goods, bribery, extortion and hampering a criminal investigation. Call a really good lawyer, Slade."

He went one better and called Robert McKinnon.

Chapter 6

From across the table, the internal affairs officer shoved the paper to rest under Slade's nose. Slade couldn't believe what his eyes were seeing.

"There has to be some mistake," he said, counting the number of digits that preceded the decimal point.

According to his bank statement, he really could write Robert a check for the replacement of that plane he had crashed and burned in the Caribbean, and it wouldn't even put a dent in his account. It would be nice if he could claim the money as his. It just wasn't. He was looking at the evidence in black-and-white.

"Are you denying this is your account, Detective Jericho?"

"I deny that all the money in this account belongs to me. It's my account number. It's just not my money. Last time I looked, which was about a month ago, I had saved close to three-quarters of a million for my retirement and another two hundred grand from the sale of my house, but

89

nowhere close to this amount. There has to be an error on the bank's end."

"No. There is no mistake. I checked." Inspector Mullins was a short man with "little man syndrome." He brandished his badge as a weapon and ran roughshod over anyone unfortunate enough to get into his path. He was paranoid and saw conspirators everywhere.

"There have been three deposits over the last thirty days, all equal payments of one million dollars. What that says to me, Detective Jericho, is you're on the take."

"So much for innocent until proven guilty." Chief Holiday said, having a difficult time watching this from behind the mirrored glass of the interrogation room. The officers standing behind him thought the comment was apropos. The murmurs in that small, darkened room confirmed that they all thought this was bogus and bullshit. The level of frustration was rising for the men who were having to stand back and watch this kangaroo court interrogation of a man they all respected.

Slade scoffed. "And I had the money put into my account here in Phoenix? That kind of money screams at you. Just how stupid do you think I am, Inspector Mullins? Besides, what in God's name would be worth that kind of money?"

"Extortion, drugs. The death of Senator Roscoe is still under investigation. How convenient that you oversaw that investigation, and it has been a botched job from the start. Let's not mention that there was some pretty costly art stolen recently. You just got back from the Caribbean. Perhaps that was more than a getaway to screw your girlfriend. Speaking of Doctor Ransom, let's talk about your girlfriend for a moment."

"You will watch your mouth, Inspector. She's not my girlfriend and has nothing to do with any of this, so leave Doctor Ransom out of this," he warned. "She lost her sister, for Christ's sake." Slade's voice boomed out across the room.

"Perhaps she's an opportunist." The little man continued to push. "Perhaps, she saw a way to capitalize."

"Shut your mouth, Mullins. I'll not sit here and listen to you disparage her reputation. She has more integrity in her little finger than we both have put together."

Mullins narrowed his eyes at Slade, sensing his one weakness. "Are you saying you don't have integrity, Jericho?"

"No, I'm saying she's good and honest. You are slandering her by even assuming she had anything to do with any of this mess," Slade said, pushing the file back over to the inspector.

Mullins sighed and ignored Slade. "The good Doctor Ransom just came into six million dollars. You have three million unexplained. Maybe you, she, and your buddies were in on that heist and sold the pieces on the black market? I also hear drugs are plentiful there in the Caribbean. You have already left the department, sold your house. Maybe, just maybe, you thought to be gone before anyone caught on to your little scheme."

"And, maybe just maybe, someone is setting me up? Have you considered that one?" Slade argued unsuccessfully. The man wasn't listening to him.

"The video says otherwise," Mullins said with just a little too much victory in his voice.

"Video of what? I'm in the dark here." Then it kicked in what Mullins had to be talking about. Slade hadn't given the video another thought after Lacy mentioned it when he was still in Dallas. "Are you talking the damaged video of the museum heist?"

Slade stood up and went to the mirror. He knew someone was on the other side. He just did not know who. "Would someone please tell me what the hell is going on? I have no idea where this money has come from, inspector.

I'm not a dirty cop. I'm not on the take, and I know less than squat about art, stolen or otherwise." He now wished he had followed Robert's advice not to said a word until Robert could get an attorney there to represent him.

"So, those expensive reproductions of several other pieces are just a coincidence, too?"

Slade sat back down. "No, as a matter of fact they aren't. Someone's going to a lot of trouble to make me look guilty. Let's not mention that it makes me look idiotic in the bargain."

Mullins shook his head. "Not going to fly, Jericho. There's too much stacking up against you."

"Why would I leave evidence like that just lying around my property? The authorities found them in my unlocked garage. Anyone could have put them there."

When the chief served the warrant to search his house, they found some forgeries placed in a pile of stuff he had in his garage. He didn't see them because, as far as he was concerned, he was giving all that away to Goodwill and hadn't looked at it since he tossed it out there. That was before he took Kristen to the Caribbean. His house was clean except for an air mattress, a few odds and ends, and a couple of old kitchen chairs. He had not decided whether to keep or add those to the category of donations. It was

Friday, and he was reporting for work in Broken Arrow on Monday.

"You know something, Mullins? I never claimed to be the sharpest knife in the drawer. However, even I can see how dumb that would be."

To intimidate him, Investigator Mullins stood behind Slade. Leaning down, he spoke to him from behind. "Maybe you just think you're above the law and untouchable."

Slade looked slightly back over his shoulder at the man. "I'm certainly neither. Only a fool doesn't realize that there's always a consequence to his actions. There's always a day of reckoning." Slade had faced that with Kristen, and it was a lesson he was still feeling the sting. "I am no fool, Investigator Mullins. If I were involved, I would never have left anything behind to incriminate myself or Kris. Nor would I have left anything to chance."

"How so?" he asked, trying to bait Slade.

"I would have seen to it that any and all evidence was destroyed and tossed out into the desert before leaving the country for what would have been an extremely extended vacation. I would also have put that money into an account that was completely untouchable. I would have seen to it that the finger was pointed in another direction using the old trick of illusion and distraction. At least that much they did right." Slade paused. "I also would never have dragged an innocent woman into this, and Doctor Ransom is innocent. She's not my girlfriend, either. There was never anything romantic between us. We kept it platonic even if there might have been a future there." Slade was now very glad he could say that with impunity. It kept her somewhat out of the mire. "Obviously, whoever planned this wasn't me."

"Why? Why should I believe you, Detective?"

Slade could see that the little weasel felt his investigation was losing its teeth, and he didn't like that fact at all.

"Because it was sloppy, and it was careless leaving a stream of evidence a mile wide. And I would be ashamed ever to take credit."

Kristen stood with her arms crossed just on the other side of the mirror. The assistant chief, Meredith Cummins, had called her in to witness this little interrogation.

"He's telling the truth," Kristen answered without hesitation and without turning to the assistant chief with her answer. She continued to observe Slade and the inspector through the two-way glass.

"How can you be so sure?" Meredith asked, needing proof-positive confirmation before she turned Slade loose.

"The face and body are very expressive, and there are signs that one cannot hide, no matter how good of a liar someone happens to be. He's under duress, and if he were lying, he couldn't hide it under these conditions. That's my expert and professional opinion, ma'am. I'm prepared to sign a sworn statement."

"And he's clean?"

"Yes, he's clean, Chief Cummins. Slade's a good cop and a good man. The other guy is a prick, and he's hiding something. He also has nothing on Slade that isn't strictly circumstantial in nature. My personal feelings aside, Deputy Chief Jericho is telling the truth. Someone is setting him up royally in an attempt to tarnish his credibility, not to mention mine. Achieve that, and all the rest follows straight down the toilet."

Meredith looked over at this doctor who had finally shattered Slade's cool professionalism. Even she had her doubts that these two had kept it platonic. However, that was not a crime and not what she was here to determine. "I guess you know the chief's job in Oklahoma is off the table because of this? They pulled the offer this morning."

Kristen looked at the assistant chief and shook her head, troubled but not surprised. Whoever was framing him was going for broke. They had to have called and tipped off the city of Broken Arrow to this investigation that was less than twenty-four hours old and completely unsubstantiated. That job was important to him. She couldn't imagine how embarrassed he was because of all this.

"No," she said and shook her head, "I wasn't aware. Detective Jericho and I haven't spoken since he came back from Dallas."

They had parted company on a cordial note. She was still professional. So was he. He had tried to call her. She had called him back, so she hadn't closed him off. They had just kept getting each other's voice mail, and she, in truth, hadn't tried very hard. She was still stinging, but she wasn't punishing him, at least not consciously. He just was not the top priority until this moment.

She had been catching up with her patients, teaching, and squaring up the remainder of Kari's estate, which she had discovered was quite substantial. Kristen knew that early the previous year Kari had found her birth mother's father. The elderly gentleman had opened his heart to the granddaughter he never knew. He had been horrified and heartbroken to discover that the couple that adopted Kari had lost custody of her when she was just two years old, and she had spent years inside the state's foster care system.

Kari had inherited close to nine million dollars from her grandfather's estate just weeks before her death, and the money had been placed in a trust for her until she was twenty-five. Kari never made it to twenty-five. With Kari's passing that money had become Kristen's, which explained the six million that Investigator Mullins alluded to in the interrogation. Too bad it just served to make Slade look guilty, too. It was just fortunate for Slade that she could also tell the assistant chief from where the three million dollars in his account had come.

Kari, for whatever reason, had set those payments up in her trust with express instruction for a specific use. The trust manager couldn't legally tell Kristen what those instructions entailed. However, she did know that, with the legal documentation in her briefcase, Slade would get off the hot seat for that piece of it.

Their being in a hotel in New Mexico was also helping to prove their lack of involvement with the museum heist. Since there was a mechanic's receipt for repairs with the date and time, they couldn't have been at two places at once. The death of Randy also helped cover them with an ironclad alibi. The local law enforcement agency had sent an affidavit that Slade was there the very evening the authorities stated the heist took place.

Slade's immigration documents into the Caribbean were covering another large chunk of time where he needed a defense. These things would help clear him of involvement with the actual heist. Not with the fencing of the artifacts.

He couldn't have handled those forgeries without touching them at some point. So the fact none of Slade's prints were anywhere on any of the items, coupled with Slade's stellar service record and the evidence of their whereabouts, had convinced the senior investigator for the FBI that Slade was being set up. The FBI was dropping the charges against him.

That didn't clear him with internal affairs, which was the reason he was sitting there in that room. However, little by little, Kristen was chipping away at the inspector's theories. It helped that Chief Holiday and Assistant Chief Cummins wanted to exonerate Slade. Her professional statement was all that Chief Holiday and Cummins needed.

As to her millions, she wanted nothing to do with the money other than paying off her mortgage and paying for her personal security, including settling the tab Slade had already racked up. With the balance, she was making arrangements for logical donations and additional scholarship funds to be set up.

Last but not the least of the reasons she seemed to be dodging Slade was a looming publication deadline that was pushed up by three weeks. She wasn't sure she was even going to meet it. The last six weeks had been odd to say the least.

She had needed breathing room to process all this. His making that bet on Kari's life had hurt her deeply, touching her very personally. However, she was past that part. He had made an error in judgment. She could cast no stone there and in truth had forgiven him before they left the island.

What she was having a greater issue with was that several other pieces of evidence had surfaced. These pieces were in addition to the key, money, and drugs that had arrived at her house. All were damning if just viewed on the surface, but none of it made any sense once she began to look logically at the evidence in a less emotionally charged context.

The carriage house explosion destroyed Kari's external drive, and the other copy never made it to Robert like Slade had planned. The courier company simply could not place their hands on it. She and Slade thought the information forever lost. However, Kari was smarter than anyone gave her credit.

What Slade didn't know was that Kari had sent a copy of all her files to her trust manager with instruction to give the disk, along with the three million dollars, to Detective Jericho if anything ever happened to her.

That had immediately raised red flags for Kristen.

How did Kari and Slade know each other?

The trust manager had asked her if she knew who Detective Jericho was by chance, and she promised to get the files to him. She planned on it but not before she finished looking through them herself.

Before returning to Phoenix, she had spent several nights deciphering the files and piecing all the notes together in a useful and more logical sequence. Kari had a distinct file system and, viewed nonchalantly, they would have made absolutely no sense to the casual observer. However, Kristen understood the workings of the human mind and, more specifically, the workings of her sister's mind. As the pieces began to fall into place, Kristen was amazed at the information Kari had managed to dredge up.

From there Kristen began to make her investigative trips to backtrack Kari's last steps.

It was the only reason she was back in Phoenix. That was what she was telling herself. Seeing Slade had nothing to do with it. That, too she kept telling herself.

She had sworn her constant bodyguards to secrecy. She was bankrolling them, not Slade. That being the case, in her mind, it was none of Slade's business that she was back in town. Chase was furious once he discovered how she had slipped out of the house under the guise of going shopping only to hop a Southwest flight from Dallas Love Field direct to Phoenix. Elizabeth had not been in agreement with keeping it from Slade or Chase and didn't keep her opinion to herself. Liz promised she wouldn't alert them.

Liz kept that promise.

Liz didn't tell Slade. She instead told Assistant Chief Cummins, who in turn told Slade, and for the last three days, he had tried to see her. Liz was no longer in her employment.

Whoever was planting this evidence against Slade was doing it for the sole purpose of driving a wedge between them and ruining him as a man.

She turned back to the glass to watch the internal affairs officer grill a perfectly innocent man. "How do we clear him, Chief Cummins? Tell me what I can do."

She owed him, at least, that much for everything he had done for her. She couldn't deny that being in love with him was not also a driving factor.

Assistant Cummins was not above using anything and everything at her disposal. "We find the man who's trying to throw us off the scent, and we'll find the bastard who killed your sister. Slade must be getting close, Kristen, if this asshole would go to such lengths to frame him."

She couldn't stand there any longer and watch this happen. She had an idea as she turned to the assistant chief. "Let me in there."

"Why?" Chief Cummins asked, furrowing her brow at this turn of events. Less than a week ago, the doctor had been ready to toss Detective Jericho to the lions if what her local Dallas police connections said was true.

"Just let me in there, ma'am. I know what I'm doing."

Chief Cummins nodded her consent. Less than a minute later, Kristen threw open the door to the interrogation room.

~*****~

Walking confidently into the room, Kristen instantly took it over.

"Inspector Mullins, I see a coaching opportunity here for your superiors. You've got nothing. You're fishing. You're shooting a broad spectrum of bullshit, hoping something will stick. It's not a good strategy to use on an innocent man. You can trust that it will backfire on you."

The look on Slade's face was not so much shock as it was one of surprise at seeing her. That same look was on the face of the investigator as well.

It was the first time Slade had seen her in business attire. She looked poised, professional, and highly polished. She looked like an attorney. She hoped that was what Mullins would think too.

"Who are you?" Inspector Mullins questioned arrogantly.

"Who I am isn't as important as why I'm here, and that is to evaluate the situation." She was going to say something entirely different, but his attitude just pissed her off, sending her in an entirely different direction instead. The last thing an interrogator wanted was someone critiquing them, standing over their shoulder, and taking notes on their performance. With men like Mullins, usually the performance fell short when faced with some pressure from an outside source over which they had no control.

He also was a woman hater. She recognized his type a mile off. He hated those women who he had to bow to in any shape, form, or fashion even more.

Kristen inwardly vowed she would see to it that he not only bowed to her but would also be kissing her ass before it was all said and done.

"Shit. You're one of *those* people," Mullins muttered under his breath.

"*One of those people?* Excuse me?" Kristen raised her right eyebrow in mock surprise.

"Inspector, there's no need to play the race card," Slade warned, starting to come out of his chair and to her defense.

Kristen firmly pushed him back down by his shoulder and then placed the palms of her hands flat on the table. She leaned over that stainless steel tabletop, looking Inspector Mullins squarely in the face and showing a lot of cleavage in the process. It was her way of saying that not only was she a woman, but all feminine in the process.

"Rest easy, Detective Jericho. The inspector isn't playing the race card. Are you?" She smiled sweetly.

No, he is too smart for that, Kristen thought. That would be just too easy to detect and not a smart career move.

Kristen looked at Slade, winked, and looked back at the other detective.

The look on Slade's face was saying *What are you doing?* She sensed his question, and she looked back at him as if to say *play along*.

"No, it's not the fact I'm milk chocolate with a little salsa and God only knows what else mixed in my blood that's pissing you off, is it, Inspector?"

He shook his head in response. Kristen could sense that he truly didn't care that she was part white and *part God-only-knows what else*.

"It's the fact I'm a dominant woman, Detective Jericho, that has this one so twisted," she said, tossing her head back toward the other man.

Slowly and with deliberate intent, she looked back at the inspector who was standing on the other side of the table. She was daring him to blink, pushing as many buttons along the way as she possibly could. "Isn't that right, Inspector Mullins? You hate me because I'm a split-tail, a woman with nice tits, and you can't stand the fact that I can pull the plug on this disaster of an investigation at any minute, and you can't do anything about it."

Mullins's mouth twitched in contempt. "You're not going to get me to admit that."

"No need," she said, standing back up abruptly. "I see that you're one of *those* people. Just give it a rest. Go make yourself useful somewhere else besides here," she said, pointing to the table, and then just as quickly she pointed to the door. "Go and leave this one alone. Crucify actual criminals with actual charges that will fly in a court of law and with evidence that can stick to something besides the creases in the bottom of my tennis shoe."

Slade was almost smiling. Kristen prayed that he kept that smile in check.

If she was lucky, he knew better because Mullins was steaming. Could Slade see that she had Mullins's number? It was about time someone put this jackass in his place, and she was the one to do it. Slade had been locked up for twenty hours and locked away in this room for close to twelve hours for a line of questioning that was getting none of them anywhere.

The inspector had come around the table and stood just a few feet from her now. "Stay out of it. You don't know anything about this case," he said as Kristen watched the veins in his neck began to beat wildly, and the pulse at his temple pounded.

"Doesn't matter," she said, shrugging. She continued to push. Looking at her fingernail polish with acute interest,

107

she completely dismissed this man's life work. She could read him and saw he was just about to ignite.

She was ready.

"You don't know dick about investigating an internal matter," he said, looking like he was about to have a stroke. He was red in the face, and Kristen noticed the way he turned the corners of his mouth down in a hard line.

"Inspector Mullins, obviously, you don't either. Your performance is lacking." She got into his personal space but did not touch him.

"Why don't you make yourself useful and go home and bake some pie, you chocolate bitch." He spat on the front of her jacket and shoved her forcibly backward with the flat of his hands. She made the most of it, stumbling backward and falling to the floor. Hitting her head was not intentional. Nevertheless, she would work it to her and Slade's benefit.

Slade rushed to her side, helping her back to her feet and then made a move towards Inspector Mullins. Kristen placed a restraining hand on his arm, fisting her fingers into his jacket and stepping in between him and Mullins. When she saw that wasn't going to be enough, she grabbed Slade by the arm and pulled him toward the door.

"Trust me, Inspector Mullins, I know a liar when I see one, and in this room, that liar is not Detective Jericho."

She could read Slade, too. She was one step away from having to call more than just the assistant chief. Slade was murderous at the moment.

"Come on, Detective Jericho. This guy is finished with you," she said, forcefully pushing Slade from behind and out of the interrogation room door.

"Get back in here! I'm not done," Mullins yelled, red in the face and ready to reignite.

Kristen jerked around to face him, taking a step back into the room. She would show no fear, not of this guy. This jackass with a badge didn't scare her in the least, not after the last six weeks that she had endured. She wasn't about to put up with his behavior. "If you had anything at all on Detective Jericho, you would have charged him hours ago. Yes, you're done, in more ways than one."

"I am internal affairs! I'll smash you like a bug so don't think you can threaten me, lady." He shook his finger in her face.

"Oh, it's no threat. You are *so* done. Assistant Chief Cummins and two other witnesses to your little outburst and loss of control are just beyond that glass," she said, pointing to the two-way mirror. His spitting on her clothing and calling her names was not a serious offense, but enough to get him in some difficult water. It might keep him busy for a while and off Slade's case. She was still undecided if she wanted to file assault charges on him for shoving her backward. Assistant Chief Cummins might just take care of that for her. Laying a hand on her wasn't smart, especially in light of the fact she was a civilian. That was something he was soon to find out.

"You should have told me out of professional courtesy, as one officer to another, that there were others behind that glass." Mullins swallowed hard.

"Oh, I'm no police officer, Inspector. That was your erroneous assumption. I'm just *one of those* people," she offered with deep sarcasm.

If she didn't miss her guess, right about then Assistant Chief Cummins was calling for a little investigating into the conduct of one Inspector Mullins.

"Oh… And, have a nice day."

She closed the door on any further comment he would have made.

Chapter 7

Slade followed her outside. Without a word, she led him out of the station and into the parking lot.

"Get in," she demanded, several yards from the car as the alarm chirped from her disarming the system with the remote.

He was compliant and didn't say anything for the first few miles. Neither did Kristen.

"Where are we going?" he asked, watching the scenery pass by him. He never liked being in the passenger seat, guessing it was a control thing. They were merging onto the interstate, heading north towards Flagstaff.

"I will be the one to ask the questions, Slade."

He was shocked at her aggressive behavior. There was something more here than she was letting on.

"All right."

I'll continue to play along, for now, he thought.

He was slightly amused. She had come to his rescue. She lied to, manipulated, and basically told an officer of the law to go screw himself. Furthermore, she had done that all on his behalf. He smiled. She was softening. Maybe she was missing him.

Reaching over, he put his hand on her leg, giving it a nice pat and rub. "So, I'm just supposed to sit here quietly while you kidnap me?"

She took his hand into hers and gently squeezed his fingers. Then she picked it up and placed it on the console, removing any physical contact between them.

All right, he thought, so maybe she's not missing me after all.

"Kidnapping was not exactly what I had in mind for you. It really isn't," she said.

His desire was for her was to crawl over the console, pin him to that passenger seat by straddling him, and lay a passionate kiss right on his treacherous mouth. Until she had removed the physical barriers of the miles and then the glass of the interrogation room, he had not realized how much he missed her. And she missed him, too.

To his surprise, with her close to him again, he knew that not only did she miss him, but she was also still hot for him. Her body was giving her away. She looked ripe and luscious, and he wanted to take a juicy bite right out of her.

Get it under control, Jericho. He had to talk to himself. He had missed her, and, now that she was close, it was all he could do not to tell her how much he wanted her back in his life.

"What did you have in mind then?"

That drew the desired reaction that she could not deny.

What did you have in mind then? His voice tightened Kristen in places she would just as soon forget. His look was smoldering hot as she recalled his words and the words in Kari's notes.

Kari had noted that he was eye candy.

Check mark in that column, Kris thought.

Kari had written, "The man is smart and smoking hot." Check and check again.

And, under different circumstances, he would be just what this doctor would order, she admitted and not even begrudgingly.

Kris pushed Slade's question aside. "I thought we just determined I would ask the questions. That was a question. Now, hush up and let me think." There was something about Inspector Mullins that did not fit. She couldn't put her finger on it exactly. Maybe Slade had some insight to her feelings.

"What is it about Mullins that doesn't feel right, Slade?"

"Everything. The guy is a prick, and he needs to thank God I didn't toss him through that mirror for pushing you."

"No, being a prick isn't all." She reasoned under her breath. "There's something creepy about him. He's covering something up, and I would bet it would shock his superiors."

"He's a shapeshifter, Kris. I'm surprised you picked up on that. He's ancient and quite good at deflecting and covering. Even I had a hard time seeing past it, and I'm trained."

Her look was one of total surprise. She wasn't sure what surprised her more. The fact Mullins was a shapeshifter or the fact Slade was trained to sense them?

"Pull over, Kristen, and stop the car," he demanded softly.

"No. I've just kidnapped you, according to your statement. Kidnappers don't cater to those they kidnap."

He was watching her profile. She couldn't hide from him any longer, and her face gave her away as they continued to head north out of town.

"Spit it out, Kristen."

He, at this point, knew her well enough to know there was something on her mind, and it had nothing to do with

Inspector Mullins. So there was no way to keep it from him, she guessed.

What Kristen discovered while digging through Kari's notes was that Slade was possibly seeing Kari, first as an informant for her investigations and then possibly as more than an informant. There were two separate entries in the files with Slade's home address and a meeting time. Kris checked Kari's cell records through the phone company's billing website to see if Slade's number ever popped up. His home phone number had come up, and Kari had called him nine times in the three days before her death. The calls were brief, less than a minute or two each time and always outgoing. Slade had never called Kari that she could determine. There were several numbers she could not trace. Those could have been Slade calling Kari back from untraceable phones, which were no longer in service when Kristen tried to call them.

Kris didn't have Kari's home phone records, needing a court order for that information. Thus far, she had not been successful in getting that order. So, just going on cell records, it was beginning to look like they had never made the connection, at least not by phone. Slade didn't have an answering machine. That piece of information she remembered from the several days she was his houseguest.

The notes on Slade and Kari were sketchy. Kari had referred to him as *the one man I can see who is honest and will get the job done if it's possible.*

Another reference to Slade *could be just what the doctor ordered for her.*

Kristen wasn't sure who *her* was in this context. Kari, probably. Her sister often referred to herself in the third person as K or KR, so it was logical that Kari might have even referred to herself as *her* instead of *me* or *I*.

Kristen was questioning these pieces of evidence and had almost from the moment of finding them. She backed away from it emotionally and began to dissect it from a rational and scientific point of view.

There had been no microexpression of recognizing Kari's picture when she showed the photos to Slade that night at the police station.

Also, his reaction was one of genuine surprise upon piecing together that Kari was also Karenna Ransom. Kari only went by her full name as an author. Everyone else who she was close to and Kristen assumed that would have included a man she was supposedly sleeping with, called her Kari. Slade hadn't blinked from the start when she mentioned Kari's name. He had unquestionably reacted when he put the two names together. Furthermore, at that

116

point, there was no need for him to deny he knew Kari. At the point that she walked into his office, they were treating her as missing, not dead.

Also, if Slade were at one point intimate with her sister, he would have shown more concern. She understood him well enough to know that he was not the kind of man to callously use a woman. If he slept with Kari, then he cared about Kari. He had been neutral, a disinterested party there to simply gather the facts of her statement.

It just did not fit that Slade and Kari were lovers or even acquaintances. It was a conclusion she had come to, not out of a desire to forgive him, or because she was wearing rose-colored glasses. She had come to that conclusion because it was logical, and it was the truth. Her being in love with him had nothing to do with it.

"Did you know my sister when she was alive?"

"Personally, no," he said, shaking his head. "I knew her name only from her articles."

"You never talked to her, met her at your home, or had sex with her?"

That stopped him for a moment. "No, Kristen. I didn't. Before you walked into my life, the last woman I was involved with was back in early February. She is a bank teller. We had gone on three dates before she threw her hands up because of my schedule."

"Just a simple yes or no will work, Slade."

Too much information, Kristen thought. She was jealous of a faceless woman who had managed to get into Slade's bed. However, with her he had only sucked her in and then pushed her away, giving her mixed signals when all she ever wanted was to be with him. Even if they could not be together forever, it would still be something she would cherish. But he never gave either of them that opportunity.

This line of questioning was one that Slade would never have guessed might take place. Obviously, there was a reason.

"No. I didn't have knowledge of her, carnal or otherwise before I saw you at the station."

He watched her profile as she nodded slowly several times. She was processing, Slade knew that much, and there had to be a reason she asked. He understood her well enough to know she wouldn't ask such a question unless there was some foundation on which to build a theory.

"Kristen, I'm sorry you got dragged into all this mess. Chief Holiday said they froze your accounts as well."

"My attorney is on it. And I understand why. I was the one who asked for your help. And, looking in from the outside, I'm the one who has been sleeping with you even if we both know that's a joke." She did not bother covering her hurt and tender feelings where Slade's rejection was concerned.

"I've tried to set that record straight and keep your reputation intact. I hope you know that you still can trust me." He reached across the car's seat to touch her hair. She moved away as far as the driver's window would let her.

Slade dropped his hand away. "Kris, listen, it is important to me that you believe in my innocence. I'm not perfect. We both know that, but I'm also not guilty of that sin."

He waited for her to respond. He wanted to tell her that he did not have anything to do with those drugs, that money, the death of her sister or the senator as Inspector Mullins insinuated. If she did not know him well enough by now to understand his moral standards, then no amount of arguing would help.

"You are innocent, regardless of what the evidence may look like to the outside world? Is that what you're saying, Slade?" She glanced over at him quickly before looking back at the road. She continued. "Are you implying the criminal justice system is full of prisoners who simply couldn't have done the crime for which they were tried and convicted but were instead framed by a sinister mastermind set out to get them? Since everyone is innocent, I don't know why we even have a justice system, do you?" she asked, blinking dramatically in mock shock. "Why not just all hold hands and sing Kumbayah?"

"Well, why not? At least, then you might let me touch you," he fired back.

He knew it looked bad. The three million unaccounted for in his account and all the odd-and-end stolen museum pieces, which the Mexican authorities had found addressed from him to a dealer in Mexico City, were all circumstantial. Still, it was damning if viewed simply superficially. There had to be some way to prove his innocence to her. He ran his palms over his face several times and through his hair in mute frustration. Then something dawned on him.

"You came to my rescue." He smiled.

"I was watching you from behind the glass."

Her statement gave nothing away. It was simply a factual reply to his statement.

"I've done nothing wrong, Kristen. I didn't steal, kill, or extort."

"Did I say you had?" She turned to look at him again briefly before turning her eyes back to the road.

"I may not have always told you everything, but I've never lied to you." He needed to know she believed him.

"No, you just kept me in the dark. You're still keeping me in the dark, Slade. And it's all in the name of keeping me safe, which is admirable but unnecessary."

"I have my reasons." Slade wondered if he would ever be able to come clean with her. He came from a world she knew nothing about. She didn't even have a clue about her own origins. He wasn't sure whose place it was to tell her; he only knew it wasn't his.

"I'm sure you do have your reasons. Few ever hide important things from someone they care about without what they feel to be good reasons. You're no different, and in your mind, they are excellent reasons."

"You're right about one thing. I do care, and they are good reasons. In Dallas before you kicked me out—"

"Oh, please." She rolled her eyes. "I hadn't taken you for one to practice dramatics. I didn't kick you out, Slade."

"All right, then figuratively speaking, you closed that door very firmly."

"I needed to think."

Slade nodded. "I can understand, but still you asked me that day if you were seeing the man I allowed the world to see. I let you see a side of my life and a part of me that no one outside the world of extreme personal security and transport will ever see, Kristen. I let you into a part of my life I have purposefully kept quiet and secret from anyone else."

Slade waited. He wasn't sure what he was waiting for at the moment. He felt that he had confessed something and was possibly waiting for the justification for keeping her dangling.

Kristen just shook her head. "For a brilliant man you just don't get it, do you? You never let me see, touch, or venture into that part of you that matters the most to me."

Her soft voice pierced him more deeply than shouting could ever have.

The only thing I'm guilty of is falling in love with you, his mind and heart yelled. Chase had said he hoped that he didn't wait for one sunrise too many to let her know how he felt about her deep in his soul. He dared not say it now. She would never believe he was sincere, instead only using the words as a ploy to get her to help him further.

"I got Mullins off of you for the time being, and your chief believes in you." She gripped the wheel tightly as she continued to drive on through the evening. "That should make you feel better."

"And what about you? Do you believe me?"

"That's two questions," she said as her answer.

"Damn it, Kristen. Seemingly you are not prepared to answer either." He wasn't angry with her, just exasperated as hell. Still, he was happy to be with her again, thinking how good she smelled and looked. Her perfume was unique and made his mind wander into dangerous territory. Thinking of safer subjects, he looked out the window. "And just where are we going?" he asked, looking at the geography and recognizing landmarks. They were in the far north part of Phoenix just on the outskirts of the city limits. He just didn't know why they were here.

Kristen took a deep breath and then let it out. "Tell me exactly where you were the three previous days before my sister died. Work backward from the moment you laid eyes on me."

"I was working homicide. You've seen my life. Where else would I be?"

"Show me," she demanded, exiting off the interstate and taking them into a less populated and more heavily industrialized area.

"Show you? Show you what? The murder scenes?"

"Yes. I need to go back over your steps and work your way backward from the time you shook my hand in that station house. Walk me through it," she asked.

"Why? Where's this going?" he questioned, furrowing his dark brow.

Kristen pulled the car to a stop in the parking lot of a closed grocery store. It was dark, and the orange light of the parking lot streaming in through the windows fully illuminated the interior of the car.

"Just tell me, Slade. Where were you, and what were you doing? You've been set up. Even I can see that."

"So, you believe me," he breathed a sigh of relief. Her belief made all the difference. Now, he just had to find who was creating this living hell for the both of them.

She nodded, placing her arms on the steering wheel and looking through the front windshield. Slade saw the moment that she let the final remnants of doubt fall away.

"Yeah." She looked at him. "Yeah, I believe you. Your station was the second station I went to the night of Kari's murder. The first one was closer. Why would I have been sent to another station?"

"Jurisdiction, Kris. Believe it or not, Kari's address is in mine."

The lines of jurisdiction were usually very clear. Those lines were set up to balance caseloads across the city. Proximity to a crime scene usually had nothing to do with the assignment or who rolled out on the call. He rolled on a murder just last year that occurred within sight of another station house. He still got the call. Boundaries were exactly that and normally if a murder occurred within the boundary, you took the call.

"No, it's more than that, Slade. Whoever killed her probably had help from someone. That help sent me to you. The only problem with that is I can't prove it. I doubled back to ask about the individual who directed me to you. No one even remembers me being there that night nor had anyone there even seen anyone vaguely fitting the description I gave them."

Slade groaned inwardly. She had been asking more questions.

"Slade, you were tagged before I ever got to the station house."

There were too many holes in her theory. It was just luck he had come back to the station at all in the wee hours of that morning. He had forgotten to pick up a form that he needed to sign and get to human resources to get his terminal leave put into place. If it had not been for that form, he would not have returned until midday. She would have come and gone, and missing persons would have taken the case.

"There was no reason for me to have taken your case," he argued.

"Not as a missing person, no, you normally wouldn't. Nevertheless, it was only a matter of time before the department would have classified her case as a homicide, right?"

"Yes," he admitted. If Kari's killer or an accomplice had sent Kristen to his station, then they already knew Kari was dead.

"Furthermore, even if you had not stepped in, the fact it was a homicide would still have placed you squarely in the line of fire by bringing the case into your department, Chief Deputy Director Slade Jericho." She used his full title as emphasis. "It just so happens that it touched you sooner rather than later."

And touched me deeply, he thought to himself. "So you think that by discrediting me it would taint the investigation?" Slade thought for a moment before debunking the idea. "There are too many variables."

"The person who wanted my sister dead would have taken that into account, Slade. They want you to take the full fall, not only for Kari but the senator as well. I can't let that happen, not to a good man, and you are a good man, Slade."

He looked at her in the shadows of the night and wondered what he ever did to deserve her. Undoing his seatbelt and opening the door, he made quick work of getting out of the car.

Kristen, surprised by his actions, followed suit, not even bothering to close the door. "Slade? What are you doing? You can't run. I promised Chief Holiday I'd keep you close."

He came around to the front of the car, and without further thought, and the consequences be damned, he grabbed her and pulled her to him. He kissed her like there was no tomorrow. He reasoned in his mind that that may be a fact. If he never got another chance, he had this moment, and he was not going to let his fear stop him because of where this kiss might lead. He released her after drinking his fill. He was like a man finding an oasis of cool water in the desert.

Placing his forehead against hers, he rested there for a moment, and then he softly kissed her brow. "Whether or not you believe me, Kris, I love you, and if I ever get clear of this mess, I swear I will make it up to you."

She stepped back to look at him. "Don't make promises you can't keep, Detective. I don't want to hear that you have deeper feelings for me. I don't want to know that the pain I feel will be your pain too when the time came to call the relationship over."

"Kris, don't say that. You don't know."

"Yes, I do, Slade. I feel confident that once you get clear of these charges, the city of Broken Arrow will be happy to reconsider their offer. There is no better man for the job than you, Chief Deputy Director Slade Jericho."

He leaned up against the car and pulled her to him. Holding her close, he kissed her again, more gently, lingering and taking his time. She felt right in his arms. This time, he wasn't going to pull away or stop, only wishing they were in a place where he could show her in a physical way how much she had come to mean to him. He loved this woman, and having her gone from his life, even for that brief time, just brought it all home.

"God, I've missed you, baby." He kissed her temple, holding her tight. "I will make this right, and if I can't keep that promise, then it's because I no longer have a breath in my body."

Kris squeezed him tighter. "I pray that day will be long in coming."

Chapter 8

Slade began to backtrack on the three previous days before their worlds had collided.

"I had just come in from a homicide on the north end of town when I heard you yelling at Rogers from across the station."

Now, it was making sense why they headed in this direction. "How did you know to come north?" He cocked his head at her, smelling a rat.

She hesitated.

"Kristen, what are you hiding from me? Come clean, lady. I know you too well."

She glanced sideways at him, sheepishly smiling. "Do you promise not to strangle me?" she asked making a face that Slade understood to be one of confidence that he was going to do exactly that.

"What have you done, Kris," he asked wanting to know but not wanting to know. He had a sinking feeling.

"I've seen the disk, Slade," she confessed, cringing just a little, fully expecting a full-blown eruption from him.

"There's another copy?" Then it sank in. "Awww, Christ have mercy on us, Kristen. That will get you killed. Where are your guards?" he asked, realizing for the first time she was entirely uncovered except for him, and he was so fried that it had taken him an hour to realize just how uncovered she was.

"I fired them for blabbing to your assistant chief, who in turn tipped you off to the fact I was back in town."

"Kris, I'm glad to have you close, but do you realize the kind of danger you're in coming back to Phoenix, especially if you're snooping around?"

"Whoever killed Kari needs me alive. I'm safe for now. Kari was following you around for some reason. She had called you several times the three days before her murder."

Ahhhhh, Slade thought, realizing that was why she questioned him about knowing Kari before her murder.

"Did she call my house or my cell?" he asked, wondering if maybe Kari had some information and was trying to get that to him somehow. It was the only explanation, and at this juncture, Slade wasn't ruling out any connections as coincidental.

"Home."

Kristen shared with him that Kari also had a couple of appointments listed in the notes with his home address. If the times checked out, he would have been home based on the time line.

"And that's why I asked if you knew her."

"And if I was sleeping with her."

He reached across the seat and ran his hand down the back of her head in mute confirmation that he understood her line of questioning earlier and to reinforce the fact he was innocent of that act, too.

He pulled his cell phone out and called Mrs. Gonzales. He asked her about the red GTO and apologized for waking her after he received confirmation that the car had been in his driveway just a day before Kari was found murdered. Slade was sleeping and hadn't heard the door if she had even knocked. In fact, she must have driven to his house and then to Sal's to drop off her car for the work on the rims. The timing would be right.

"Slade, what if she was trying to give you something before she left town?"

"I guess it's possible." He and Kristen had come to the same conclusion. He just had no idea what that something could be; information, evidence perhaps, but of what?

The murder scenes from the three previous days before Kari's death had turned up exactly nothing except the fact that the last murder's location was a building that looked strikingly similar to the interior of the museum. It was a similarity that was completely lost to everyone except Kristen. The video of him from the museum heist was filmed at the murder scene and then somehow superimposed over some other footage to make it look like Slade had been at the museum the night of the robbery. The expert analysis would prove her theory and then backed up by immigration records showing he had been out of the country.

The call to his chief had the evidence already on the way to Washington for unbiased examination and analysis.

"To your house," Kristen said, tossing Slade the keys at the last scene.

He nodded and headed that direction. However, he made one stop along the way. His house was virtually empty at this point. The movers had all his things in storage until he could find a place to live in Broken Arrow. He had already closed on the house with the new owners and was just awaiting the final walk-through before he moved to Oklahoma. Too bad that plan had gone to hell in a handbasket.

The disappointment of losing the chief of police position was not as great as he would have first thought. It had been liberating once he got past the shot to his ego.

Pulling into the parking lot of the upscale hotel, he wanted this time with her if she would have him. He potentially would pay the ultimate price for this. He prayed it would be worth it.

If she were hurt again in the future, he could never heal her. It was forbidden to heal your mate. He wanted to do more than just make love to her. He wanted her for all time. It could prove to be a very selfish act. However, with Kristen, he was feeling quite selfish.

Additionally, if the Council of Violations ever found out he had made love to her with the bonding ritual performed, then they both could be put to death even if she did agree willingly. He would gladly make that sacrifice; however, it potentially placed her life at risk.

He reached over and across the console, pulling her to him. He kissed her deeply, passionately pouring his true feelings into that kiss.

"Kristen, let me be with you. I know I've been a jerk at times, but I have loved you all along." He kissed her on the forehead and then softly on her lips again. "Can you trust me that I've had my reasons?"

"Slade, I trust you with my soul, and I trust you with my body," she answered truthfully.

"But do you trust me with your life?"

If he did this with her, she would have to trust him to keep her alive should the council ever truly decide to press the issue.

"Do you see a bodyguard around?" She looked around emphasizing the fact she completely placed her faith in his ability to keep her alive. "What I'm not sure of is if I can trust you with my heart."

He hesitated to answer her and then waxed poetically, thinking about what Chase had said to him back in Dallas. It fit.

"Lend that which you cherish most unto my safekeeping. I will shelter it as if it were my own."

She closed the gap between them, crawling over the console and into his lap her suit skirt rode high on her thighs. "It belongs to you, Slade. The question is what are you going to do with it?" she asked as her bottom hit the horn. They laughed just before he kissed her.

~*****~

Chase was sitting on his patio back in Dallas, enjoying one of his more pleasurable lady-friends and a glass of fine aged scotch. He had come away from that kiss in the woods with more than just a memory of Kristen.

Feeling the heated breeze cross over his skin, he felt in his mind Slade stake claim to her.

"About damn time," he smiled and breathed a sigh of relief. His obligation would now no longer include marriage to her. Still, it might not have been all bad.

Chapter 9

Pulling into the driveway, Slade went around to the back, parking the rental behind his personal car. He relinquished his department car when he terminated from the force, and it had been in the body shop for several weeks before the murder. A suspect rammed the car while Slade was questioning the suspect's wife.

Slade unlocked his car and sat briefly on the passenger side as he pulled the flashlight out of the glove box. He began to look inside the car, thinking Kari might have left him something in there. Turning up nothing useful, he was beginning to look around the foundation of his house and under the decking of the porch.

There, secured in a clear plastic baggy was a memory card he had never seen belonging to a camera he didn't own. He hadn't yet reached for it when he felt a dark force pushing in on him.

"Uh—Slade?" Kristen softly called from behind him.

"Yeah?" He turned, hearing something in her voice. "Oh, shit."

Detective Green had resurfaced and was holding what Slade could only assume was a loaded gun to Kristen's head.

"Green?" Slade was shocked. "What the hell do you think you're doing?" Why would this nineteen-year veteran be holding a gun on Kristen?

"Put your hands on your head, Jericho. You know the drill. Interlock your fingers." Green waited for Slade's compliance.

What else was Slade going to do? The bastard had a gun to Kristen's head, and the silencer would keep anyone from knowing that they were dead until the sun came up in the morning. If Green happened to see the memory card, then by morning he would be gone along with any evidence the card may have on it. If they were lucky, that piece would remain hidden.

"Slade, open your jacket very slowly so that I can see your piece. I believe you wear it under your right arm."

Slade complied, slowly pulling the jacket open to reveal the .45 he always carried under his arm in the shoulder holster.

"Now, Kristen, please relieve Slade of his gun and pass it to me. Ahhh, ahh, ahh. Sloooowly," he warned when he saw her moving. "Now, with your left hand, please pull it out by the butt with two fingers. Don't get your finger anywhere near that trigger or your boyfriend gets it between the eyes."

What was she supposed to do? Green was pointing that same gun at both of them. She reached into Slade's blazer and pulled out his firearm that Assistant Chief Cummins had gladly given back to him.

Slade gave her a look that told her not to do anything stupid. He would get them out of this mess one way or another. His mind was racing and coming up with nothing useful. Detective Green had seen him in action for far too many years to fall into the trap of getting close enough for Slade to disarm him.

Green waved his hand toward her once she pulled the firearm out of its holster. "Come on, we do not have all night."

Kristen gave him a murderous look to which he merely smiled in return and forced the gun tighter into her back.

"Good girl. Now, into the house," Green commanded roughly.

Slade had never felt as helpless in his entire career as they entered the back door of his house. It was empty of almost all of Slade's belongings except for the mismatched chairs in the kitchen and a few boxes of personal belongings stacked neatly in the corner of the living room.

"Grab that chair there and sit down, Jericho." Green tossed the cuffs to Kristen and turned the gun on both of them. "Cuff him to that pipe," he ordered, pointing to the natural gas line for the stove.

Kristen hesitated and looked to Slade for answers.

Slade nodded. "Just do as he says, Kris. It will be all right. I promise," he said and ran his hand down the side of her face in a reassuring gesture.

"Isn't that special? Makes me want to hurl my last cup of coffee. Now, get away from him and sit over there." Green pointed to the other chair that he moved far enough away from Slade to where they could not touch, but he could still monitor both of his hostages with relative ease. He held the gun to her head. "Now, wrap your hands behind the chair," he ordered, moving behind her to cuff her hands. He did not dare turn his back to Slade.

"Do whatever you need to do to me. Just don't hurt her, Bill," Slade asked with his voice level and composed. What he, in fact, wanted to do was kill this bastard.

"You like her, don't you," Green asked with a little hint of surprise. "This is good. It will make you, even more, compliant."

"Please, leave her out of this, Bill. Kris has nothing to do with whatever this is all about." Slade was not above begging.

Green furrowed his brow. "Oh, Slade, she has everything to do with this." Green ran the barrel of the gun down the side of Kristen's face, forcing a desperate sound of fear to emerge from her lips.

"Leave her alone!" Slade resisted the urge to jerk at the cuffs.

"What?" Green asked in mock surprise. "Leave her alone, just like you leave everything alone?" Detective Green shook his head as he held them at gunpoint. "But you never were one to leave well enough alone, Jericho. You always had to get your man. Your honor was at stake to keep a perfect track record on the force."

Slade could see the unadulterated hatred oozing from this cop.

Kristen's mind began to clear. "I remember you. You were the one who insisted I go to Slade's precinct station."

She told Slade that she had taken the cab to the first station house from the apartment. "He pulled in behind me just as I exited the cab, asking if he could help me. Did you follow me from Kari's? The timing was just too coincidental for you to have simply timed it at the station.

You were watching. Now that I think about it, I didn't ask for help; you approached me first. You used me as a tool. You used me to get to Slade. Why frame Slade for all this?" Kristen asked with tears swimming in her eyes.

"He was getting too close to the truth," Green said.

Slade continued to tamp down the urge to pull at the restraints and to try to reach the shut-off valve at the base of the wall with his foot. Green cuffed him to the central section of the natural gas line for a stove that was no longer there, and one false move could spell disaster. If he broke that pipe, the possible explosion would kill them all. He vowed his next house would be all electric.

"And what's the truth, Green?" Slade asked, never betraying his fear for Kristen's life.

"You're the hot-shot detective, Slade. You figure it out." The venom was thick, and Slade was almost sorry he had provoked Green, who still had his gun pointed at Kristen.

"You're somehow tied up in the senator's murder." Slade felt certain. "Green, look, man, we can still work this out. Just put the gun down. Don't throw away your career."

Green was holding Kristen by the hair, pulling her head back, with the barrel pointed at her temple. "You think I care about this freaking job when my life is now worth squat? Things would have been fine if you had just left the senator's death alone."

Slade remained quiet. He needed the facts and asking questions wasn't going to gain him anything. He kept his mouth closed, knowing most people hate silence and will talk when nervous. It was Interrogation 101.

"Levine's bitch, Yalena, killed Senator Roscoe to make way for Levine in the special election. You were supposed to be off the streets, and the investigation of Senator Roscoe was supposed to go to me. It was supposed to be an easy job, going unsolved with all the evidence tainted, lost, or destroyed. I was paid handsomely for that result, and your valiant detective over there made that tough, always taking charge, always insisting he come along or sending Lacy in his absence."

"The senator's death?" Kristen questioned. "Levine? I remember the name from Kari's notes. What does my sister have to do with the senator?"

Green turned her loose. "She didn't. Not at first."

"So, so… I'm confused."

Green shrugged. "I needed Slade out of the way."

Slade could see how for Green it was just that simple in his mind. An innocent sacrificed for the greater good and to cover his corrupted ass in the process was alright.

Slade was mute, taking all the guilt onto his shoulders. He saw where this was going, even if Kristen had yet to connect the dots.

Green continued to gloat. "I thought to myself, now what a great way to get Slade out of the picture and off the senator's case. If Slade were wrapped up in you and chasing Kari's killer, he would leave the senator's case to someone who I could manipulate."

Green told them how at first he was going to have Slade take the fall for Kari's murder. He reconsidered, realizing very quickly he would have a hard time with that setup.

"Ruining his career was better and easier, and it would get him off the senator's case. His precious honor means more to him than anything."

Not anymore, Slade thought as he looked over at Kristen. She was everything to him, and he had to keep them both alive. If the last few hours had shown him anything, it was the fact he could never leave her, not now. He had found the love of his life, and he was damned if he was going to let a two-bit, crooked cop take that away. If he was willing to stand up to the Council of Violations for the right to possess her as his mate, then this guy was nothing by comparison to those scary bastards.

"I don't understand," she asked, looking back and forth between the two men, and wondered where and how this all tied together.

"I befriended Kari," Green offered smugly. "She was quite naive. It took nothing. I dropped a few hints, gave her a few facts."

Slade saw her questioning look, begging him for answers.

"He was one of her sources, Kris." Slade remembered seeing Detective Green's name in the files, but he didn't think much of it at the time. Green was a common name. There were several names of cops in her records as sources, not suspects. "So, Green? Did you feed that poor girl just enough to keep her on the hook?"

"Yeah, and to get her into bed, too."

Even with her hands tied, Kristen tried to come up out of the chair. He put the barrel of the gun firmly between her eyes.

"Sit! Down!" He pressed that barrel firmly enough to her forehead that it left a red ring visible on her skin. "I didn't succeed. Kari wanted nothing to do with me, and any time I tried to make a move, that damn cat of hers that she took everywhere with her would get in the way. Now, I said, sit—down!"

Kristen complied. Green turned his attention back to Slade.

"Kari talked about her sister, showed me photos. I took one look at Kristen, Slade, and I knew you would not be able to resist. I was right." Green shook his head smugly. "You are pathetic, Jericho. You fell for her like a ton of bricks. Unfortunately for me, I killed Kari before Levine informed me she had been snooping around in his business and needed to see what she knew."

Slade noted the tattoo on his hand for the first time. "You took the other half of my key ring off my desk at work and stole her keys from Sal's. You made copies of her house key, attached it to that keyring, and, then sent them to Kristen's house in Dallas. You let yourself into her apartment."

"Oh, very good, Detective," Green said with false praise.

So that is how it happened, Slade thought. Lacy's theory was right, and that explained how there were no red flags raised with any of the guards in Kari's complex.

Slade shook his head. Green had played him well. "You offered to look at the surveillance tapes further covering your tracks. You also had the ability to get back into the apartment after I changed the locks. No one would have thought a thing about you coming back."

"I didn't go back. They beat me to it. However, I know Kari kept all her notes on an external drive and that they didn't find what they were looking for when they did go back. I need that drive, Slade."

"If you did not go back and ransack the place, then who did?" Slade asked, alarmed that there were now three sets of players and all were in it for different reasons.

"It was Levine's soldiers." Green was hiding out from Levine and his group. Getting that drive was the only thing that would keep him alive. "Where is it?" he demanded, putting the gun back to Kristen's head. "For the love of God, Slade, if you have it, hand it over. If I have it, Levine might not kill you by some small chance. You have no idea who or what that man is, Jericho."

"He doesn't have it, you moron." Kristen lashed out, kicking him hard at the kneecap.

"Shut up, Kristen! Don't tell him a damn thing!" Slade snapped at her. The less she told him, the better off they would be.

"Then where is it?" Green moved the gun to Slade's head.

"Th explosion destroyed it," Slade said, just as Kristen was saying that they had made copies.

Green went red, and then white in the face. "Then we're all dead."

Then Green went silent. He dropped to his knees, falling face forward on the kitchen tile, a knife protruding from the base of his neck. Slade caught movement out of the corner of his eye and looked over at the kitchen window just in time to see Bobby jump down from the sill where he had been watching and listening.

Looking back to the direction from where the knife was thrown, Slade and Kristen saw a woman standing in the doorway of the living room, covered from head to toe in black leather and lace.

She was wearing skintight leather pants tapered to her shapely ankles. The corset had red satin lacing up the front. It artfully showed off more skin than it hid. The elbow-length lace gloves were designed to allow for her long, graceful fingers to flow out the ends, showing off perfectly manicured blood-red nails. Long dark-brown hair flowed flawlessly to her waist. Seductively, she sauntered into the kitchen.

"My, my, my… What do we have here? A little game of bondage, perhaps?" Her laughter was seductive and a deadly sound for any unsuspecting. Even Slade had a hard time resisting the pull.

Slade noted how beautiful the woman was, yet his intuition was telling him this was no ordinary woman. There was something ugly, deeply disturbing, and dangerous lurking beneath that mantle of external beauty and sexuality.

"Who are you, and what do you want," Slade asked.

"You're the detective. You tell me."

"Yalena, I presume," Slade said with as much calm as he could muster.

"Ahhh, see? Not so hard after all," Yalena said as she continued to make her way into the kitchen.

Slade heard the slow tap, tap, tap on the tile floor. He noted her heels. Those stilettos were probably similar to the ones that had so callously made the mark on Kristen's photo back in Kari's apartment.

Green may not have gone back to Kari's apartment, but this dangerous she-devil certainly had. Yalena straddled his lap, pressing her leather-clad body into his. It was a misguided attempt to arouse him. Wrapping her arms around his neck, she moved in for a kiss. Reflexively, he turned his face away.

"Ohhhh, a challenge," she purred, never taking her eyes from Slade. "Lorenzo, show him what can happen if he defies me again."

Lorenzo slapped Kristen hard across the face, breaking her delicate skin and bringing blood at the corner of her lip. It smeared bright red against her cheek. The blow was hard, sending her and the chair toppling sideways to the tile of the kitchen floor. Kristen hit hard with nothing except her body to break her fall. Slade heard the air rush out of her lungs. Slade also heard the crack of her skull as she hit her head on the tile. Then, he heard nothing.

Lorenzo put his foot firmly against Kristen's neck. One good push and her neck would snap as she lay there momentarily dazed and defenseless.

Yalena laughed softly. It sent a chill down Slade's spine. This soft and flirtatious sound did not fool him. Having come to the conclusion this was no ordinary woman, Slade knew he needed to tread lightly in these waters. Yalena was a shark patrolling cold, deep waters, constantly on the prowl for unsuspecting prey. She would order Lorenzo to kill Kris with the snap of her fingers and never think twice about it.

"Now, shifter, shall we try this, again?" She firmly grabbed his face and squeezed painfully. Much more pressure and she would shatter his jaw. She had Slade at a disadvantage. They were extorting his weakness of Kristen's safety, and because of him, she was being pulled deeper down a path and into a world that would kill her if not negotiated carefully.

"Fine! Yes, just don't hurt her." Slade pulled hard against the cuffs that kept his hands behind his back. He was now confident that instant death by an explosion would be preferable to death by her hands. Yalena was a vampire, and a kiss from her could be deadly if not carefully navigated. Vampires were just like snakes; some were venomous, and some were benign.

This bitch was toxic to the core.

She was the equivalent of the pit viper and the adder in the snake world.

"Kiss me, shifter, and make me a believer," she commanded, only inches from his ear, having already run her raspy tongue straight up his jugular vein from his collarbone to his earlobe. "Otherwise, your little half-human pet will slowly die at the hands of the flesh eaters."

"Too bad you are forbidden. You smell good enough to eat, and if I had a heartbeat, it would be beating just a little faster from the heady smells and tastes you can certainly give to me. Even your sweat is deliciously laced with fear, adrenaline, and a heady mix of hormones."

"Yeah, I'm a real delicacy." Slade's sarcasm was thick. Still, he knew that she was not prepared to die for taking just a single taste. He was forbidden fruit by vampire law. Even she had more restraint left than that, and her sense of survival was still intact and stronger than her desire for this rare treat. Or he hoped.

So, she knows I'm a shapeshifter, Slade thought.

He wondered if she knew he was a symbiotic healer or was she just guessing? Slade wanted to look at Kristen, but the vampire bitch held him firm. Yalena closed the gap between his mouth and hers, still holding him firmly by the jaw. Kris's life depended on him giving the snake what she wanted. If she wanted a kiss, then a kiss she would get. However, nothing ever comes for free, and there was something he would extract as payback.

Slade swallowed the bile rising in his throat, quickly realizing she had recently fed. She still had the metallic taste of fresh blood on her lips, something that was abhorrent to him. He pushed past it for Kristen's sake and kissed her, pouring himself into that action. If she wanted him to make her a believer, then by God, he would. She just didn't say what kind of believer, and before this would be all said and done; he would make her a believer all right. That belief would come right before a royal screw-you.

However, he had to keep her engaged, so he kissed her while mentally removing himself from the act itself. He heard her soft moan at his ability to turn even the most hardened creature all soft. He laughed in his mind. Knowing she had recently fed meant she had the capacity to bleed. Just before pulling back, he bit her hard, drawing blood and taking that vile, polluted cocktail into his mouth. He felt his system revolt. It felt like poison with the strength of arsenic was being delivered straight into his bloodstream. The pain she caused him for that act of drawing blood was excruciating as she hit him in the solar plexus, breaking several ribs in the process. The end result was worth the price.

Just as he had pieces of Kristen in him, he now had her, too. Once he got close, he would now be able to track her. It would be harder to track her while she was awake, but once she was asleep, he would always know where the bitch made her nest.

Lorenzo's scowl told Slade that he was Yalena's nest mate, which was the equivalent of a personal pet, snack machine, and sex partner.

"Now, where were we," she asked Lorenzo after wiping the blood from her bottom lip with the tip of her finger and then dabbing it on Slade's lips.

Slade spit to the side as much in defiance as a necessity. His system could only take so much of the toxins before he would be rendered unconscious from the neuron inhibitors. His mouth was already going numb.

Yalena stood up, hissing at the insult, and on impulse scraped her nails across his face, leaving deep gashes that instantly began to ooze and stream with fresh, warm blood. The sight and smell nearly sent her over the edge as she growled deeply in her throat. "Blood for blood, shifter," she breathlessly said just before she licked him. "Mmm, heady," she said, closing her eyes and throwing her head back at the quick rush and momentary high.

"Pray, Yalena, the council never discovers your mistake." Slade smiled in triumph.

Yalena retracted in horror as Kristen jerked at her cuffs. "Get away from him, you filthy bitch! He's mine!" she yelled, visibly not caring that cuffed she was vulnerable.

Yalena snapped around and hissed like a snake, baring her fangs at Kristen.

Kristen sucked in her breath. "What kind of Alice-in-Wonderland nightmare am I in here, Slade? Get me out of here!" Kristen began to fight in earnest, kicking at Lorenzo, inching her way to the back door to flee. Her fight-or-flight instincts were in overdrive.

"How quaint. Just look…" Yalena said patronizingly, "we have a pathetic, little fighter on our hands."

Then Yalena hardened, and Slade felt the air leaving the room. "Now, Lorenzo, do your job and shut the little bitch up before I have to do it for you." She slapped him hard across his face.

Lorenzo dared not fight back. "Let's get on with this, Yalena. Yuri is waiting for us," Lorenzo wisely reminded her as he rubbed his cheek but did his mistress's bidding.

Slade watched in horror as the man shoved a muzzle in Kristen's mouth and a hood over her head. Pulling her up off of the floor, they dragged her kicking and screaming, backward through the kitchen door.

"Kristen!" Slade yelled, fighting against his restraints as they dragged her through the open back doorway. "Don't you touch her, you filthy bloodsucking bitch!" he warned Yalena as he pulled himself to his full height. "If she's harmed in any way or dies, so will you. I have no more reason not to go to the council, Yalena." Few knew that there was power in using a vampire's name, especially if you have shared blood.

He saw Yalena's brief hesitation as she weighed whether to call his bluff. "It's no bluff, Yalena. If one hair on Kristen's head is touched, I'll know."

There were pieces of him floating inside Kris now too. The final bonding was rapidly progressing as their DNA melded together. He had laid claim to her, and there was nothing to undo the wheels that he had set into motion. The domino effect was building speed, and before much more time passed, their genetically programmed responses would be forever set.

"Twenty-four hours, Jericho. Get any and all copies back to us, and I might let her live. Fail me, shifter, and she dies," she paused, tapping her fingertip to her cheek, "or maybe I'll just make her an open bar for the rest of the group. We'll be in touch. Ciao." She waved her fingers and then blew him a kiss.

Watching helplessly in revulsion, Slade fought against the handcuffs as Kristen disappeared into the night. If he shifted now, he would be dead before he could rematerialize. Yalena would shred him to pieces when he was at his most vulnerable. He could not leave Kristen without even the faintest glimmer of hope. He had to hold his cover and pray his plan of tracking her worked.

The second the door closed, Slade turned to mist, slipping soundlessly out of the cuffs. They fell to the floor with a resounding clatter. By the time he got out the back door, Kristen was gone. All he could see were taillights heading into the night.

The next thing he did was call Chase, the only other man he knew who hated vampires more than him. And, after tonight, Chase might have to relinquish that title because Slade was quickly heading for the front of that line.

Chapter 10

The last five hours were nothing short of agony for Slade.
It had taken Chase three hours to get from Dallas to
Phoenix and another two to organize the groups necessary
to wage this battle looming ahead. That elite team was still
assembling. There was one more that had yet to arrive, a
deep undercover operative with personal and intimate
knowledge of the vampire networking system on this side
of the Atlantic. Chase had never met the woman personally
but according to Richard McKinnon-Callahan, a cousin of
Chase's who lives in Austin, Texas, this woman also knew
her way around the European connections as well and had
helped him on more than one occasion in the past.

According to Chase's sources, something had stirred
the nests of dozens of vampire colonies. They were
converging in New Mexico close to Carlsbad in droves,
almost like their version of Woodstock. That meant another
two hours at minimum to get there from Phoenix by jet.
Best case scenario only left them fifteen hours to find and
retrieve Kristen once they touched down in New Mexico.

The men gathered around the card table. Chase had started a game of poker just to help distract the men until the last person arrived. There was nothing else to do until they had the last pieces of intelligence.

Slade posed the question to the small selected group as they sat in the war room. "Green said something to the effect that we have no idea who and what Levine might be. Do you suppose he is something other than human?"

Time was ticking, and they all felt the walls closing in, yet planning was critical to the success of any mission.

They were inside a warehouse in Scottsdale, and from the outside, it looked like nothing more than a light industrial building set on five acres and nestled in the center of a cluster of three more just like it.

The inside of that building was a totally different story.

Soundproofed, secured, and containing a full firing range, it also had racks containing munitions, body armor, and other tools of the deep-black operations trade, which McKinnon-Bride Security was known to do on a contractual basis.

Chase shrugged at the question of Levine's origins. They were at a loss and had gone over several different scenarios. Nothing fit together.

Chase pondered the question further. "Given his associates, it's logical that he's not human but something *other than*. However, vamps don't usually play well with others. I've seen no indication that Levine is a bloodsucker, either. If he is, then he's a whole new breed of cat."

Slade took the silver-plated blade and expertly landed it in the body-shaped board on the wall fifteen feet behind Chase. "So where does that leave us, if he's not a vampire, not shifter and not human?" Slade asked as he pulled the knife out of the wall. They had to know what they were up against if they had the slightest shot in hell of getting Kris out of that viper's nest alive.

"I can help." The female voice came softly from the darkness.

All eyes turned to the voice coming from deep in the shadows of the back part of the room. The turning of all those heads accompanied the rattle of weapons, the sound of them being pulled, and the clicking of rounds being charged into chambers.

"Ah, boys and their toys..."

~*****~

Chase growled. He could smell her, feel her, and sense her as the fine hairs on his body stood on end. She was a vampire, forever young, forever beautiful, and ten kinds of deadly.

He recognized her instantly from his research.

Sophia Romeo had resurfaced after forty-five years. She sauntered into the midst of the group, totally confident in who she was. Her soft, ultra faded jeans, cowboy boots and light pale-pink sweater did not fit the goth persona a lot of her kind seemed to prefer for whatever reason.

"Senator Levine is demon-spawn," Sophia offered the answer to the question on all the men's mind.

"Ahh, demon-spawn." The light came on for Slade. It made sense to him. "A nasty mess of genetic material…"

"And, usually not tolerated by the vampire community." Chase finished the thought, all the while wondering if she were friend or foe.

Sophia continued to make her way into the inner circle. "Not usually tolerated, no. However, he was raised by one in the elite caste who found him as a child, took pity, and kept him alive." She held up her hand as she saw mouths opening. "And, before you ask, no one has ever quite figured that one out, least of all me."

"What do you want?" Chase asked, silently pulling out his blade. Surely this was not the final player they were waiting on, not with Robert knowing how he felt about them. Robert would never be so bold as to expect him to work with this creature. He had never kept his animosity secret, especially from his brother.

"I want the same thing you do, Chase," she said as she came around behind him, leaning over his shoulder, reaching for the cards he had put facedown in front of him on the poker table.

"Seeing you dead?" Chase asked dryly, briefly wondering how she knew his name.

"I'm already dead, Chase. Ooooo, nice hand," she said, flipping over the cards, laying them faceup on the table. "It's just too bad that you can't finish playing it."

Chase saw her reflection in the mirror across the room. Something passed across her face before she quickly hid it from view. Sophia was a woman. It didn't matter if she was not a human woman any longer. He could still read her. She hated who and what she was, even more than he hated who and what she was.

Interesting, he thought.

"It's revenge you want. Why?" Chase questioned, more curious about this newcomer than he wanted to be.

She placed her hand on his shoulder and looked at him. "It is not important why it's revenge I desire, Chase. It's just important that I do want it and that I'm willing to help you to get it. Purely selfish, I assure you, my love," she said, running her fingers through his hair and sitting down in his lap. He jerked away earning him her sultry laughter.

"So… Your enemy is my enemy. Therefore, we're friends?" Chase asked. He was also wondering how she had gotten past the dogs. There was something he was missing.

She stood up and walked around the table, turning over the other four sets of cards one by one.

"Not quite that easy, but I'm willing to lay aside my hostilities. I can help you. You can help me. It's business because it can't be a pleasure." She stopped and paused for dramatic flair. "Let me see if I can remember it correctly. I am 'a creature of the darkest sort and have no feelings'. At least according to your website."

Chase recognized his words.

Again, there was something there just under the surface that Chase couldn't see, but he sensed almost like a flash out of the corner of his eye. He knew it was there, but when he turned his head it was already gone.

"Chase, we have to listen to her. If she knows something, then we have to deal," Slade finally chimed in after taking in this interplay between the two. "What do you need from us in return for your help?" he asked, turning to Sophia.

"Oh hell, no! I'm not placing my trust in her." Chase stood up, no longer comfortable with Sophia to his back again. She could just as easily slit his throat as look at him, and anyone in this room could not stop the speed at which that action would occur.

Sophia sighed. "There is great potential in you, Chase, but you have hardened your mind to the possibilities. I grow tired of the games, and I'm running out of time, which was quite ironic considering I potentially could live for thousands of years. So, just shut up, Chase, and listen to me. This situation isn't about you. It's about getting Kristen back, in some semblance of her current self. It is immaterial if you want my help or not. I had hoped you would reciprocate. Your cousin Richard said you probably wouldn't. Regardless, I will still help you and pray we all live to see Kristen again."

"Please, don't listen to him, Sophia. Help us. Help me find her. What do you know?" Slade asked, wishing Chase would dial back the level of hostility that Chase was putting off into the room.

Sophia nodded. "Kari's shapeshifter, the one you call Bobby, made a deal with Yuri Azanov to bring Kristen to him in exchange for the name of the man who killed Kari. However, we all know how that attempt to kidnap Kristen ended."

"Yeah, we do," Slade said. "It nearly killed her."

Sophia agreed. "When the kidnapping failed, it set into motion another plan. Yuri talked Yalena Lopez and Lorenzo Salazar into doing his dirty work and getting Kristen to him. Yalena agreed to exchange Kristen for the information on the portable drive for Levine, which Yuri got from the overnight package in New Mexico. He was the one who killed your agent in that hotel room."

"Yuri has the disk?" Chase asked, wondering how he knew about the drive.

"No, he's no longer in possession of the disk. He didn't have it long enough to see what was on it either."

"So Yalena gives Kris to this Yuri guy in exchange for information he no longer has?" Slade felt a prick of fear trail down his spine.

"Yalena has absolutely no intention of giving Kristen to Yuri. Still, she must play along until she can confirm Yuri didn't view the disk."

"Who is this Yuri?" Slade asked, questioning who all the players were in this game.

Chase recognized the name. "Yuri Azanov—one deadly son of a bitch that every violations bounty hunter from Afghanistan to Zimbabwe would love to get into their crosshairs."

"He's a soldier of Levine's," Sophia offered. "However, he has a separate agenda."

"Every vamp has his separate agenda, Sophia." Chase had sat back down next to her. Something about her was familiar, and for whatever reason, beyond Chase's wildest comprehension, he did trust her. So did Slade. Not that they had a real choice. "Where is he holding her? Do you know?"

"He has her in El Paso. They're just across the New Mexico border, south of Sunland Park."

Sophia let them know that the last she heard, Yuri had not informed Levine that he had Kristen, and that was regardless of the fact Yuri was given a direct command by Yalena to bring her straight to Levine with as little delay as possible.

"Yalena knew that he wouldn't. Otherwise, she never would have turned her over to him. What's Yuri's angle?" Slade asked.

Sophia darted her eyes to Slade. Chase watched her closely and wondered if she noticed that there was something different in Slade's demeanor. Slade's agenda was vastly different from his or the other men at the table. For Slade, just like her, this quest was personal.

"Just how personal is this mission for you?" she asked.

"Just about as personal as it gets. What about Yuri?" Slade asked again.

"Yuri craves her blood and her body. He desires to bond with her before he turns her over to Levine. He's just dense enough to think sex is all it takes to bond and that Levine would never kill him or the nest mate of one of his high-ranking officers."

"That can't happen. I'm already bonding to her,"Slade said.

Chase felt Kristen's life was not as valuable as it once was, and he knew that Slade would blame himself for touching her. Still, the thought of her bonding with the likes of Yuri or Levine turned his stomach. Better she die as Slade's mate than live as the slave of another. Slade would probably agree.

"Then, if you're fortunate, and she's lucky, he'll kill her quickly once he discovers she is useless to him in his personal quest. If not," she said and closed her eyes, shaking her head, envisioning a fate worse than death, then continued, "then her fate is worse than mine."

Chase understood that there were two kinds of vampire. Those born to it and those made into it. Those born vampires were less volatile, more even in nature, and lived relatively normal lives even if that life was extremely long. The natural-born creatures were more human than monster, and it was simply a genetic mutation that created them.

Those born vampires were able to survive on food, not just blood. They could marry, have children, and hold down regular jobs. They weren't the walking dead but were living organisms. That much he did know. They are not made by the painful alteration of their DNA structure that happens to the others.

Those made into vampires were creatures of varying nature. Their lives were a living hell if their maker did not do it right and take responsibility for their creation and development. The young ones often became insane from the hunger and internal struggle to stay alive if not raised in a nest that nurtured and guided them down the very dark path of the early years and out into the light.

What are the chances of that? Chase wondered. The thought of vampires and light in the same sentence was just not something he chose to accept. There were those occasional day walkers, but most were creatures of the night.

"So even if Yuri can't bond with her, he'll likely still try to keep her in exchange for the information on a disk that he no longer has?" Chase asked, leaning back on the back two legs of the folding chair with his arms crossed over his chest still hiding the open blade running along his forearm.

"Maybe. It has been many years since I saw Yuri last." Sophia shifted her attention to Slade. "Your healing of Kristen sent quite a stir through the colonies, Slade. Yuri is quite obsessed with Kristen now that he figured out what she is. Even if he cannot bond with her, her blood is still worth millions."

Sophia explained how it had been centuries since the old ones had smelled such a sweet bouquet of blood and pheromones. The result was the gathering that they had gotten wind was occurring. Between Slade's and Kristen's blood, the treat would be sweet indeed. Many had traveled the globe just to have a single drop of Slade and Kristen's blood placed on their tongue.

"It is the rarest combinations for the race, and many would die for the prospect of a single taste. They will

170

continue to gather in the sacred place regardless of the risk of discovery."

"Yeah, we heard," Chase agreed and was glad that mystery was somewhat solved as to the gathering of the masses. He knew the catalysts but not the final result of half of the Vampire Nation gathering in one small New Mexico town. That could never be a good thing, and no good would come as a result of it.

"Once Yuri released Kristen's scent, the scouts were dispatched straightaway, and Levine was ordered to find her and immediately turn her over to the council. I have never seen him quite so angry. He will eventually turn her over, but he needs her for personal reasons."

"So why does the council want her?" Slade asked.

"Aside from the high it offers, her blood is a rare ingredient in an ancient alchemist's recipe. The mixture is an elixir that relieves the burning of the thirst for blood in the new ones."

"And, would then allow for the creation of thousands with little need of guidance on the part of the maker. Oh, my, God! The council, with Levine's help, wants to create an army. We will never allow that to happen—ever. I'll nuke the whole council first." Chase was resolute that army was never going to happen.

"Not the whole council, just one councilman," Sophia answered as she leaned against the tall shelf containing the very items necessary to end her life. Absently, she fingered the wooden arrow lying beside the crossbow. Sophia looked at the silver tip attached to the wooden shaft. "Death at three hundred and fifty yards," she said under her breath.

"And you? How do you fit into all this?" Slade looked intently into her eyes.

"What the hell?" Chase could not believe his eyes.

Without them ever blinking, Sophia moved so fast that they did not see her set down a huge diamond, and a plastic case containing the CD Slade had copied. Both were now resting on the table in the middle of the poker chips.

"The Shake? How did you get it from the museum?" Slade asked. "And what about the other artwork?"

"I didn't take the art, Slade. I had nothing to do with that. It was Levine and his group. And the Shake was never put in the museum vault to begin with."

"So, you have had it for how long?" Chase wondered how she had kept it secret until it dawned on him that the Shake family stood to gain millions from its loss.

"By request of Oliver Shake, I've had it for over forty-five years. I was the gemologist who verified its value and authenticity. At the time, it wasn't worth much on the open market. Oliver wanted the millions the future market would give his great-grandchildren. Let's face it, when he had me appraise it, the diamond was worth less than a third of what its value is now, even in modern terms of inflation. The sixties and seventies sucked as far as the economy went. By tucking it away for the last forty-five years and surrounding it with an air of mystique and hype, he created superhigh intrinsic value that far outweighs market value."

"So, by having a fake already under glass and in the museum without ever having to risk the real thing, the insurance will pay. The real diamond remains in the safekeeping of a very long living and trusted confidant, and generations later the diamond resurfaces," Chase said putting the pieces together. "I see an issue there. The insurance money that was already paid would have to be reimbursed once the diamond resurfaces. The Shake family wouldn't be able to retain ownership, and a diamond like this is just too recognizable unless someone reshapes it. That action would devalue the worth significantly." Chase just could not see the logic behind the decision to have Sophia safeguard the diamond. "It makes no sense," he said scratching his head.

"Oliver had a special clause built into the insurance policy stating that should the diamond ever be lost and after a period of seventy years resurface, then the diamond would revert to the Shake heirs, and they would not be held accountable for the insurance already paid out for the previous claim. So the clock is ticking.

"You have got to admire the patience of the breed," Chase said, figuring that living for millennia gave you that luxury.

Sophia heard the comment spoken softly under Chase's breath. "Yes, we do have patience. We can take a hundred years just to decide on a color for the curtains. I just upped the ante, boys. Levine wants the information that he thinks Yalena will bring him. I think if it were just Yuri we could persuade him to take the diamond as consolation for not having Kristen as a mate, but the councilman wants Kristen for her blood, and he is fully expecting Levine to deliver. You have to let him deliver her to find who is behind the plot to create the army of new vampires."

"And what do you want, Sophia?" Chase asked, wondering exactly where this strange alliance would end up taking them all.

"What do you think?" she asked, picking up the crossbow and testing out the draw.

"Levine's head on a stick?" Slade knew the answer.

Chase and Slade both knew that would only be for starters.

"Ahhh, that would be nice, too," she said, bringing that bow to the side of her cheek and expertly placing one of those silver-tipped arrows square and center of the bull's-eye over one hundred yards away.

Slade stood up, abruptly knocking the chair out from behind him. He quickly reached for his weapon. His eyes hardened into a slit of black onyx. "Yalena! You filthy bloodsucking bitch!" Slade yelled into the night.

"Slade?" Chase questioned the look crossing Slade's face. The man was dangerous.

Sophia was deadly calm. "They have tasted Kristen, Chase. They have opened her veins. I can smell her even from this distance. So will the council."

Slade was as cold as hardened steel. "I warned Yalena, Chase. I freaking warned her! Now, it's war."

Chapter 11

Yuri pulled up from Kristen's leg and wiped the traces of
blood from his mouth. "She's useless to me."

Yalena watched as Yuri stormed around the room after
taking his fill of Kristen and stating his shock at how
quickly the hollaquine was bonding with the shifter. Slade
could not have made his claim that many hours ago.

"I can still smell the sex on her panties and the inside
of her thighs. I can't bond with her now. Her DNA is
already altering at lightning speed," he said, throwing a
lesser nest member against the wall who had tried to come
too close.

Her blood was amazingly sweet to taste. It was rich,
smooth, and velvety. Her blood was supposed to be
superior to any and a high unmatched anywhere. She tasted
exquisitely rich; the best he had ever sampled. Yalena
could taste the difference in her blood cells, and the high
she produced was electric. By sheer force, she and Yuri had
to control the nest from totally draining her dry.

Yuri was standing by the bed where Kristen had been
forced to lie facedown with her skirt removed. He was too

smart to let them bite her on the neck. Instead, choosing her inner thigh, more easily disguised. They had all fed from her, leaving her almost unconscious from the loss.

Yalena defended their mistake.

"There is still hope, Yuri. She might not be of use to you as a nest mate, but the shifter is a healer. Do you realize how many years it has been since the council has seen one? Just think of it, Yuri," she purred into his ear, running a finely manicured nail down his one good arm. "You could even promote past Levine with this treasure to present to the council. And if she bears the shifter a child, then that child will be of great value to his high councilman's desires."

"How do you know her mate is the healer?" Yuri questioned.

Yalena could see that he was wondering what else she knew and was not divulging, and he probably thought that the alliance with *this she-bitch* was risky, even if necessary. *He is right to wonder,* she thought.

"It is a logical deduction, Yuri. The scent of her blood reaching the inner chambers and the murmur running through the council are all good signs there is a healer involved. The fact Slade has not been away from her for more than five minutes lets us know it's not the McKinnon man. And other than Slade, Chase is the only other man who he let close to his precious hollaquine."

"Hmmph, I guess if there is an upside it would be the shifter. She unquestionably is useless to me other than as a hostage. I certainly can't keep her for food, no matter how delicious she is. That blood would be too addictive."

He may be older than me, but he's not operating on all cylinders, Yalena thought. She marveled that he was still alive and had advanced as far as he had in Levine's ranks. Muscle did have its place, and Yuri was a prime example of that. Brains were optional it would seem.

"Yuri, Yuri, Yuri…" Yalena shook her head, patronizing him. "Your anticipation and then the subsequent disappointment of not being able to have her as a mate has clouded your opinion and ability to think this through clearly."

"I've never been clearer, Yalena."

She ignored that remark. "I know you are disappointed, and the greater the anticipation, the harder the letdown. Just because you cannot bond with her doesn't mean her blood isn't still effective for the councilman's purposes. The reward will be astronomical."

"Maybe so, but I'm eager to dispose of her. Her kidnapping was worth the risk as long as the possibility to bond with her was viable. With that plan dashed the risk is too high to hold her for very long. Levine is not going to be happy with us as it is."

"Patience, Yuri. Patience. We need the copies of the disk," Yalena said as Yuri paced the small one bedroom apartment, probably praying that she did not ask him for the disk he'd managed to lose.

"Do we have to hold her until the detective gets us the other copies of the drive?"

"Yes. Once he does, then you can take the disks to Levine and the shifter and the hollaquine to the council as an offering." Yalena softly closed the bedroom door behind Kristen's unconscious body. It was getting close to dawn, and it had been a long night. She was ready to sleep. "Keep a watch on her, Yuri. If you deliver her, the council will defend you against Levine. Keep that in mind."

~*****~

Kristen drifted in and out of consciousness as the night turned to day. Yuri had secured her hands to the bed frame with nylon rope. After working her head onto the pillow, she finally managed to get the blindfold off of her eyes.

With that obstruction gone, she was able to see her surroundings.

The apartment was fairly still with just a few quiet snores breaking the silence. It was dark but not pitch-black. Even with blackout curtains on the windows, she could make out shapes in the darkness. The occupants slept in various chairs and on bedrolls. They were obviously not vampires.

It was ten in the morning according to the digital clock resting on the nightstand across the width of the bed, the bright green of the numbers lightly illuminating the darkened bedroom. She had been kidnapped around two the same morning. That meant Slade had sixteen hours to find her before Yalena would do whatever it was she had planned.

Now that she could see, she quietly worked on her restraints and managed to get one hand loose from the edge of the bed. Stretching her hand across the bed, she reached for what she hoped was the cordless phone resting on the opposite nightstand. She almost had it as her fingertips rolled past the edge, just touching the handset.

It was too far out of her reach.

Then, taking the bandana that Yuri used over her eyes, she fashioned a noose using her one free hand and her teeth. She would try lassoing the antenna to turn the handset forty-five degrees.

After almost giving up, she tossed it one more time and managed to get the edge of the bandana on the phone. "Yes!" she whispered in triumph after thirty minutes of trying. Gently, she turned the phone, holding her breath. She didn't want to drag it off the bedside table. Stretching her full body to the point of pain, she curled her fingers around the precious object. Covering her head with the pillow to muffle the sound, she prayed for a miracle.

She dialed and prayed someone would answer. She heard the first ring and then another before the pillow went flying from her face.

~*****~

Levine threw the phone against the bedroom wall, shattering it into pieces. Snatching Kristen up by her arm, he pulled her through the bedroom door and barked orders to clean up the mess his men had made.

It was the law: you never left anything of evidence behind.

Other than Yuri, who he would deal with later, the others were as expendable as vermin vampire or human wannabes. All were very replaceable in the grand scheme of things, especially in light of the fact he was soon to have a whole world-dominant army at his disposal. He wouldn't create them, but once the high councilman fashioned them, they would be his to command and the high councilman could kiss his elite ass goodbye. He would take over the White House first and work his way out from there.

Yalena had told him where to find Kristen. At this point, Yalena had convinced him the disk was all but secondary. Once he had the army behind him, the fact that he was a thief, bedfellow to the Mexican cartels, and a slave runner wouldn't matter in Washington or anywhere else for that matter. He would rise to be the leader of the new world order, an order that he would fashion.

Years of planning, whispering treasonous words, and planting seeds of greater glory in the high councilman's ear was coming to fruition, and the councilman didn't even have a clue that Levine was the puppet master.

The smug bastard had always felt he was so superior to Levine's messy bloodline. Well, the days of human superiority was quickly coming to a close. He, Thomas Levine, was about to turn his creation full force against them all.

Chapter 12

Slade looked at the number on his phone. It was a far West Texas prefix.

"Hello?" he asked.

The only thing he heard was Kristen scream his name just before the line went dead.

"Son of a bitch!" Slade yelled, then wheeled to head to the exit.

Chase grabbed Slade before he could get two steps past him. The fight that ensued was fierce. It took four men to get Slade under control, and the look Chase received was a cross between a man and a beast. There was something untamed in Slade. Chase felt the beast lurking just below the surface. Slade's mate was in danger, and the primal drive was there.

There was no way Chase was letting Slade loose until the man centered himself. Slade needed to get back as close to neutral as possible. Given the circumstance, that was going to be tough.

Chase was the voice of reason. "They have moved her already, Slade. Our best bet is to go straight to Carlsbad."

"All I can hear, Chase, is Kristen screaming on the phone before it went dead."

Surprising everyone, Sophia placed a loving hand on Slade's arm. "If it's any consolation, Slade, they must keep her alive, if for no other reason than to keep the council from seeking retribution," Sophia offered. "She is too valuable to use as a food source. And, as a hollaquine, she is already a mystic so they cannot turn her."

"That doesn't mean they can't torture her. Do we even know who has her?" Slade paced like a caged tiger.

"I do," Bobby said as the guards dragged him into their midst and tossed him into the ring of Chase's men.

"Let him go," Slade commanded. "Spill it, Bobby."

"You know this guy?" Chase asked, still holding his gun pointed at the scruffy young man.

"Yeah, Chase, meet Bobby, Kari's pet shifter."

Bobby got to the point with Slade. Chase and Slade felt that there was no time for anything else. "You saw me in the window at your house in Phoenix."

Slade nodded.

"I got the information I was looking for—who killed Kari. So with Detective Green's death, I got the revenge I was after. I crawled into the car in Phoenix when Lorenzo and Yalena first took Kristen. I have tried to keep close tabs on her. It was the least I could do for Kari's sister. It was Levine who came this morning with his security detail and snatched her from the apartment in El Paso, killing everyone except Yuri in the process."

"How do you know all this," Chase asked.

Bobby's informants had called him right away with the information.

"Was Yalena with him?" Slade asked, checking the clip in his gun one more time. It was an unconscious gesture on Slade's part, and it let everyone know that the payment due the double-crossing-she-bitch was going to be painful. Slade loaded that gun with bullets laced with a cocktail of a genetically produced virus designed to incapacitate. It was the equivalent of a vampire tranquilizer, which rendered them immobile but not unconscious. The second ingredient was hydrochloric acid designed to penetrate flesh and explode on impact. If a soldier could not sever the head quickly or destroy the heart, then the acid would eventually kill them as they lay there with the full knowledge that they were dying.

It was cruel and crude, but the best defense they had at the moment. Weapons against the vampire were hard to develop, and few worked effectively. The benefit to this was it struck fear into the vamps, something not easily done. It was a very useful deterrent to those who might not routinely cross over the line. It made them think twice, and often that was all it took for them to realize the act was not worth the cost.

Bobby shook his head as he straightened his shirt. "No, Yalena was not with him this morning, according to my sources, but she was the one who told Levine where to find your mate."

"Where has he taken her? Do you know?" Slade had calmed considerably. He continued to pack his bag with the tools and weapons necessary to wage the war for Kristen's release.

Bobby nodded. "I have a strong suspicion from listening to them talk. I have Sam on it. I'm expecting an answer soon." The shifter was on *shaky ground* with this group. After all, he had tried to trade Kristen. The act had almost killed her. For that he was remorseful.

"Who's Sam?" Chase asked, wondering if Sam was his accomplice in Kristen's aborted kidnapping attempt.

"Sam's one of mine. I have come to offer you assistance, Slade. It started out as revenge for Kari's death, and I'm sorry about trying to kidnap Kristen. It was nothing personal."

Slade was furious again as he grabbed Bobby by the collar. "Nothing personal? Tell that to Kris, you matted fur ball. How do I know you won't try that shit again?" he said forcefully, letting him go and putting the barrel of the gun between Bobby's eyes.

"That debt has been settled with the death of the man who killed Kari. I loved her, Slade. I could not let her death go unavenged."

Chase sounded suspicious. "So, if you have settled your score why are you here?"

There were three levels of shifters. Each breed was more evolved than the last. There were those who had no hard-and-fast social skills or language skills. They seldom formed bonds or communities. The best way to describe them was that they were similar to butterflies that start out as caterpillars and shift into the winged beauties. The highest level was an ancient race called the Maji almost at the brink of extinction. Along with the Maji were those rare individuals, like Slade, who had a tendency to be from the lines of Native American descendants, and they ranked up there with the Maji and humans in cognitive superiority.

Shifters of Bobby's breed were somewhere in-between. They were capable of love just as Bobby had loved Kari. As a rule, they were very discrete and stayed out of the way. They flew low and under the radar most of the time. This willingness to help was a break in their normal behavior.

"I respect that you are suspicious, Chase, and I have my reasons for exposing our presence to you and the vampire. I have gathered a small army and more are coming as we speak."

"This is no game, Bobby. Your people will die. They know that?" Slade had to be sure he understood.

"Slade is right, Bobby. There will be casualties," Chase said, punctuating Slade's statement.

"Yes, we get that, Chase. We're tired of living as second-class citizens. We are sick of the vampires treating us like we are nothing more than food. We have tried to play the game, Chase. I know some will die. However, we can no longer sit on the sidelines. Here in America, the vamps change the rules at their own whim and to their own favor. We will no longer tolerate this behavior, Chase. I cannot allow what Levine and the high councilman are planning. It would significantly change the balance of power, and that balance must remain. If that power shifts to the vampire nation, the impact on all living creatures would be disastrous."

Bobby had a point, and everyone standing there got what the exact point happened to be. Absolute power corrupts absolutely, even in a creature such as a human who possesses a moral compass. Place that same power into the hands of a creature without the capacity to feel remorse and the result would be apocalyptic.

"So you know what his plans are?" Chase asked, raising a dark brow.

"You have long overlooked our usefulness, Chase. There is very little we do not know." The phone buzzed on Bobby's hip as a text message arrived. He looked at it briefly and then closed the phone. "That includes where they have Kristen. Pack the rappelling ropes. We're going spelunking."

Chapter 13

Thirty miles outside Carlsbad
New Mexico

Fourteen hours had already ticked off the clock since they took Kristen.

Five hours after Bobby got the tip of where Yuri was holding Kristen, Chase and Slade belly-crawled to the edge of the canyon to have a reconnaissance look at what they were up against. The sun was still high in the sky, and the heat was rising right along with it.

It was a brilliant location, much to their disappointment.

"The bloodsuckers aren't going to make this easy for us," Chase whispered as he edged closer to the rim.

Not that either expected anything less from a race that had the ability to take years to plan even the minutest of affairs. This gathering was obviously nothing minor if the number of cars lining the desert were any indication. The large tarps designed for desert warfare were camouflaging them.

"Cha-ching," Chase said, noting that the cost to keep this gathering secret was not cheap by any stretch.

Slade spoke his thoughts and wondered if the military satellites that covered this sector might pick up on this, and if they did, would it raise any flags? From this angle, the desert looked like the parking lot of the last major league game he attended. By his estimation, if there were only two occupants per car, the attendance would measure in the thousands.

The team could only venture a guess where this mass was all hiding.

"Wherever they were, it has to be subterranean," Slade offered.

"There is just one small problem with that theory," Chase said as he inched closer to the rim. "There is no evidence of any cave of any size in these parts, not on any map that I've been able to get my hands on recently. Smaller caves are dotting around, but none of any magnitude."

"It would have to be enormous to house this many," Slade agreed. Carlsbad Caverns, some thirty miles away, could take on this group. However, that was not where this group had landed. "I suppose it's possible that there is a yet *undiscovered* mega-cave."

Chase nodded. "There's also nothing to say that any hiker unfortunate enough to stumble on this site would ever be allowed to leave."

They both knew what that meant.

"There!" Slade pointed to the shadowed opening, revealed now that the sun was higher in the sky and not casting the canyon into dark shadows. The contrast was very clear now.

"Damn…" Chase cursed softly under his breath as he brought the binoculars to his face. Distance to the entry was well over three hundred yards. The seven guards that he could count were just the beginning of the obstacles.

The hideout of the gathering was very defensible with its entry hidden from the casual eye. It would require that the visitors have foreknowledge of exactly where they were going.

Slade wondered aloud how the message as to exactly where to show up was getting to those gathering.

Chase never took his eyes from the binoculars. "Cell service would be my guess. Even ancient creatures can learn new tricks. I'd say approximately three hundred and forty yards."

Slade quickly did the mental calculations, taking distance, wind, and angle into consideration. "Easy sniper range but not the best move."

The cave opening located at the termination of a blind canyon would require them to squeeze past sheer vertical cliff walls that were barely eighteen inches apart from side to side in some places. There would be no quick retreat should it become necessary to fall back. That was simply not going to happen. They were not going to leave themselves without a way out.

They talked about several different plans of attack. Chase felt he could snipe some of the guards with rifle fire but not all. That would only result in sounding the alarm. Both men agreed that the quickest and most silent but also the most dangerous way into the cave was to drop in on the guards from the top of the rim just above the opening. They had to take them out one by one and leave nothing behind as a red flag that anyone had been there penetrating their defenses.

Upon first inspection, the cave only had one way in and one way out. However, given Chase's vast experience and expertise in caving, he felt certain there was more than one entry to this cave system. If it were closer to dusk, the bats would be the best clue to an alternate opening. They could not wait until dusk. Kristen simply did not have that kind of time, and neither did they.

Bobby eased his way along the rim to rest beside Slade. "The guards are probably drones or human pets, given they are out in this glaring sun. No vamp would risk this UV exposure even with an umbrella and SPF 300."

Chase and Slade agreed. That made it easier for them to eliminate the opposition, at least at the cave opening. Inside was another matter. Who knew what they might face once they got inside.

Bobby offered the best alternative yet. "Let my men take them out for you. Any newcomers to the gathering would have no way of knowing that the guards were not friendly until we already trap them inside."

Chase and Slade met eyes over Bobby's head. They had to trust him. He had an advantage they did not. Shifting could come in handy if given the right circumstances. In this instance Slade's talent was useless, and Chase was not capable of shifting at all.

"What do you have in mind?" Slade asked, wondering what was on this shifter's mind and what strategy he might think to deploy given their current situation.

"Not all of us are as benign in our construction as I am, Slade."

Slade nodded. "Well, whatever you have up your furry sleeve had better be quick, silent, and lethal. Anything else is useless."

"I'm on it. Just be ready to drop over from the rim at the mouth when I give the signal. Within thirty seconds, you will never know the cave was ever guarded by anyone other than me and mine."

Slade timed it.

Twenty-eight seconds after the first scorpion unleashed its venom the whole lot was unconscious, dragged out of sight, and probably no one would ever find them in the vast expanse of the desert.

Chapter 14

Passing into the mouth of the cave, they were now walking through what was millions of years ago an ancient seabed. It consisted of thin layers of limestone laid down in a process taking millions of years when a shallow sea covered the Americas. The tunnels were dark and dank having been carved out by groundwater knifing its way through fissures and fractures in the bedrock of limestone—a process that took millions of years more.

Relative humidity was at ninety-eight percent as water dripped from saturated surfaces, leaving slime in some areas. The air was cool in contrast to the hot and arid desert condition awaiting them just beyond the opening.

Slade and Chase could hear the voices coming from within the depths. The crunching of their footsteps on the gravel walk, which was not something they had expected to see, almost masked those voices. The tunnels paving in some areas and gravel in others, starting at about fifty feet inside the mouth of the cave let the team know that the vampire used this cave on a routine basis. No doubt the occupancy with this much renovation and modernization.

Farther down the pathway, the electric lights were a surprise. They should not have been.

Bobby and his team were nowhere Chase or Slade could see. They were doing their job by taking out any resistance they encountered as they made their way through the maze of tunnels. Leaving bodies like breadcrumbs for the extraction team to follow, Slade and Chase, along with the others, were now only feet from the main chamber doors.

It was a massive obstruction, and they had no way of knowing what stood beyond without simply opening the door. That was not an option that would usually be high on the list in either man's book. The options were few, given their circumstances, and none of those options were very appetizing for any of them to swallow. They were outnumbered, outgunned, and charging blindly into the fray. There were few choices and no time to come up with a better plan of attack.

Chase hesitated at the massive doors. They were at the point of no return. "I don't know about you, Jericho, but this will be one for the books if we get out of here alive and in one piece."

Slade nodded. "It has been a pleasure," he said, shaking Chase's hand. Slade had to get Kristen out or die trying. Those were his only two options, and if he could not get her out alive, he would sacrifice her life before letting these creatures have her for their twisted ends. It would be the merciful thing to do for her and humanity.

Chase had that look come over his face that Slade had seen once before. It was a pure adrenaline rush. "Now, what you say we kick some vampire ass? The last one out buys the beer."

"Deal," Slade agreed.

Chase had his hand on one door handle, and Slade had the other when a voice from behind stopped them cold.

"I wouldn't do that just yet, not if I were you."

No one had sounded the alarm to the presence of this woman.

For Chase, that could only mean one thing.

Caroline.

Chapter 15

Chase closed his eyes and dropped his chin to his chest. He did not turn around. "Six billion people on this planet and I have to run into you?"

"Now, my pet," she purred, "there are worse women you could bump into, especially in New Mexico, in a dark cave, and with only a six-inch plank door separating you from a room full of vampires. I'm sure they would not treat you to the same warm welcome I would have had you crossed my threshold." Queen Caroline of the Vampire Nation cooed from behind, her provocative and delicate accent a surprise.

"You know her?" Slade asked in fascination at the interplay between these two.

Chase knew the vampires had caught them. Nonetheless, Slade sensed no fear in him. Chase still had his back to her.

Odd, to keep his back to the enemy, Slade thought. Maybe this exotic beauty was not the enemy after all.

"In a manner of speaking, yeah, I know her."

Why was Slade not surprised?

Chase did not comment any further and finally gained the nerve to turn around and look at her.

"Why are you even here, Caroline?"

It had taken years for the bitterness Chase felt because of her to subside. Now, he simply felt contempt. Not a lot of difference in the emotion except that he had managed to transfer all his animosity he felt for her individually and direct it at the entire race, not just Caroline or whatever she was calling herself these days. He was spreading the wealth, so to speak.

With her exotic looks and royal bloodline, she was still just a beautiful as ever. Not that she would ever change, Chase corrected himself. He reminded himself who and what she was, and what she had done to him eleven years ago at the tender age of twenty in that Somali desert.

Still, this queen of the bloodsuckers did do him a favor. It had opened his eyes and given him insights into the workings of the vampires' minds and their black, corrupted souls.

Come to think of it, he mused, Caroline was no different from his ex-wife. That cheating bitch also had a black soul, not to mention the morals of a stray dog. He could not speak to Caroline's morals.

Nonetheless, he could speak to her black heart. So, maybe it was not the vampire in Caroline that gave her the black and cold heart, but the fact she was a woman. He wasn't interested in finding out either way.

"It has been a while, Chase. I was beginning to think you had forgotten I even existed." Caroline sounded almost hurt.

"Truthfully? I had forgotten about you."

That's a lie, Chase thought. No man ever forgets this woman once his path crosses hers. Some don't forget because of the pleasure, others because of the pain. For him… It was a large dose of both.

Caroline looked him up and down. It made him feel like she had just stripped him bare. Emotions buried deep bubbled to the surface.

"Your reasons for being here, Caroline, *do not* include me."

"Your Majesty," Sophia said, bowing to her queen, stepping in before it went any further with these two. "I am glad you were able to make it in time."

"Sophia, it is a pleasure to see you again. Chase, darling, Sophia called me, and I am here for the same reason you are, love. The hollaquine is a curiosity. I wish to see her firsthand."

Chase resisted the urge to roll his eyes at her flimsy excuse. "I'm not buying that, Caroline. If you wanted to see Kristen, you would have simply commanded her to be brought to you. After all, you are the high queen bee of this debacle." The sarcasm dripping from Chase was palatable.

"Can I not wish to see my loyal subjects who reside on this side of the Straights of Gibraltar?" Caroline toyed with him.

Chase blocked her. "That voice may work on everyone else, but you're talking to me, Caroline. So just cut the crap. I know for a fact you haven't given this group over here in the Americas more than a passing thought since the fall of the Mayan empire."

"You wound me deeply, darling."

"Why now?" Chase snarled, grabbing her by the shoulders, narrowing his eyes, and totally oblivious to the fact her guards were only feet away and could kill them in the blink of an eye.

Chase was barely aware of the sharp intake of Sophia's breath and the fact Slade was taking in this encounter.

"Interesting," Slade said to the fact none of the guards moved to come to her defense.

Chase did see something there in her expression as she looked up at him—regret, sorrow, or longing perhaps?

It has to be the play of the dim lighting, Chase thought.

"I saw an opportunity to accomplish several things. Seeing the hollaquine was one. Reminding my subjects that I'm still here and that I am still their queen is simply a bonus."

Chase growled. "Stop playing games and wasting my time. What's the real deal? What are we walking into here?"

"Fine," she said, shaking her head in exasperation. It sent the hundreds of jewels in her hair twinkling like small flames of white-hot fire. Someone painstakingly wove those gems into her hair with golden threads no thicker than a spider's silk. Even in the weak light of the entryway, her hair gleamed blue-black like a priceless piece of highly polished onyx. "I could never pass anything by you, even when you were the tender age of twenty."

"Answer my question, Caroline," Chase demanded.

"There is some clever character who for the last several years has been trying to undermine my throne. I don't take kindly to assassination attempts."

Slade was watching them carefully and noticed the thin lines of anger creasing the edges of Chase's mouth. There was history between these two, and it did not take a rocket scientist to see what the history entailed. She was a breathtaking female in form and grace. Her sex appeal went beyond her looks to a deeper challenge and a sense of danger, and Chase was—well, Chase. Slade could see where a young and impetuous Chase at twenty years old would go for broke with this woman. Vampire or not, they had been lovers at some point along the way, and it had apparently not mattered to Chase at the time that she was queen or vamp. What was also clear was something along that same path had changed Chase's attitude, and Slade's guess was it was Caroline.

"Someone is trying to kill you?" Slade asked.

"I do believe that is the definition of attempted assassination," Caroline said, cutting her eyes over to Chase.

"How close have they gotten?" Chase found himself asking. He was more engaged than he was letting on.

"Close enough," she retorted. "Help me find the bastard who isn't playing nice, and I'll help you live to see your next birthday," she promised, running a finger down the Velcro fasteners on the front of his flak jacket. From his vantage point, Slade could see it was a caress Chase found to be just a little too familiar and a lot unsettling.

"No," Chase said with little or no hesitation.

Taking her hand into his, he removed it from his chest. Obviously, he did not want to be this close to her again in any context, not as a woman and certainly not as the monarch of this nasty lot. Slade could understand. He knew his vampire history and what she was capable of doing, regardless of the fact she was a very tiny woman, small boned, and by all appearances fragile.

He was no fool. She was the real deal.

These facts all creatures needed to keep in the forefront of their minds when dealing with this ancient queen.

This woman was a daughter of the line of Cain. She was a natural-born queen. She was a killer trained from her birth to lead an army and defend herself and her subjects.

She just chose not to lead that army into battle.

That did not mean she would never change her mind.

"Tell me, Chase, exactly what is your plan once you open this?" she asked and waited for his answer while leaning seductively against a door that would lead them to an uncertain future. "You've got nothing, do you?"

The distress in her voice is indisputable and real, Slade thought as he watched her draw her brows together in concern.

Chase shrugged those large shoulders, letting it all roll off as he had a tendency to do. "We'll figure it out as we go."

Having to think fast on their feet and having a plan was *absolutely* necessary, but flexibility was the other fifty percent of the equation, seventy-five in this instance.

Slade watched diligently as the queen studied them. All traces of the flirting were gone and in its place was a genuine concern for all their safety, not just Chase's. She had looked at the whole team, acknowledging them as individuals. That said a lot to Slade. She was not as self-absorbed as she led others to believe. He found that thought-provoking.

"Even if you have not given my memory pause and have managed to forget me, I have followed your triumphs and tragedies through the years, Chase. You have never been one to, how you say here in America, simply wing it. You are gloriously impulsive and magnificently impetuous in many things, which I find delightful. That being said, a mission has never, ever been one of them. I do not advise starting such a course of action today."

Caroline began to motion for four of her guards to remove their clothes and for Chase, Slade, and two others to change.

Slade could feel the window closing on Kristen's safety net. Soon they would do what they brought her here to do, and once that started there would be no turning back the hands of time.

"Chase, we're wasting precious time here. If Queen Caroline is offering help, then broker the damn deal and let's get on with it."

Caroline placed a hand on Chase's arm. "Listen to the hollaquine's mate, Chase. The benefits to you... Well, will be more than just saving your sorry hide." Caroline sweetly smiled as she watched the men change into the royal guard uniforms.

"Fine. Terms?" Chase grimaced, pulling on the garments. "God, these stink," They smelled foul to him, reeking of vampire sweat.

Slade sensed that Chase was to the point of feeling that the hands of time were ticking just as he did. If it meant sacrificing his resolve never to be this close to Caroline again, then so be it. He and Chase would just deal with the fallout once they got Kristen out alive.

The queen stepped closer to Chase again, invading his space, trying to keep him off-kilter. "I need you as my personal guard. I need you... I need you to help flush out the traitor."

Chase shook his head firmly in the negative. "I will not be your guard. If I'm to get to the bottom of this, I can't be a visible feature in your life. It must be subtle, behind the scenes, and I'm not naive anymore, Caroline. You taught me a thing or two, and I'll do this under one condition."

"That would be?" Caroline looked slightly back over her shoulder as a loud eruption of clapping filtered through the massive door. Someone was giving a rousing speech. The narrowing of her eyes spoke volumes to Slade. The fact the council had not invited her was not sitting well with the queen regent.

"One month is all you get of my time." Chase held up his finger. "One and that is all."

She balked. "That is simply not enough. One month with an auto-renewal up to eighteen months, with two such optional renewal terms," she countered.

"No renewal. If I can't find and flush this bastard in one month, then he's far superior to my skill. And no sex, glamour, or trickery, either. You keep me alive and safe while I'm in your service, and I promise I will kill the bastard myself for putting you in a position to ask for help from the one person you know hates what you stand for." Anger rolled off Chase. They all felt it.

Slade recognized the hurt that shot across Caroline's face. She was not quick enough to cover it. Even if she was older than even the written word, she was still a female with more delicate feelings than she might let one believe.

Caroline stood just a little taller, refusing to be intimidated by this human male whom she could snap into two pieces with little to no effort if the mood struck her. It did not matter how much history she and Chase shared or what he might have meant to her. Slade could respect that.

"Very well, Chase. We have a deal. I concede to one month, but I will not give on this one point. You must concede to be my chamber guard during the hours in which I sleep. I'm most vulnerable then."

Chase shook his head, refusing to concede this point to her. "What part of 'not being your guard' did you not follow me on?"

Caroline turned to Slade, sensing that he had the most to lose in this affair. Sophia had spared no details, and Caroline must have realized that Slade was deeply in love with his mate and would do just about anything at this point to save her. Apparently she had no qualms about using that. "Slade, talk some sense into him."

"Chase, for God's sake, quit screwing around! How bad can it be? Just give her what she wants." Slade could just imagine the fear Kristen was feeling all the while they were brokering a deal that was stalling just because Chase didn't want to be a guard, which was what he was trained and paid to do.

Caroline huffed in an exasperated sigh. "The man is impossible and quite conceited," she said to Slade before turning back to Chase. "I don't need your service in my bed. I have what I need in that aspect of my personal life. So, you are off the hook. What I don't have is someone reliable. I trust you, Chase, even if you hate what I stand for. At least, I know where I stand with you. I always have. If you are going to kill me, at least, I know you would not do so while I sleep."

"Are you so sure of that?" Chase narrowed his eyes.

"Yes, positive." She nodded. "You prefer to stake a girl through her heart while she sees it coming."

With that, she tossed the door open wide.

"No going back now," Slade said as he followed Caroline first into the room.

What he saw made him sick.

Chapter 16

A hush fell over the room as Queen Caroline entered,
pushing her power out in all directions in front of her. Her
powers of persuasion and captivation were enormous, and
she enthralled the weaker, more simpleminded of the crowd
with no effort whatsoever.

The others capitulated because of the surprise and awe
of having the one true queen in their midst. She was the
living, true descendant in the direct line of Cain. Caroline
was Cain's only legitimate daughter and older than time
itself. Taking the throne directly from her father, she was a
born vampire and the oldest of their kind.

Many had thought her only a myth.

No one, save a very select few, ever saw her.

They were taught to believe in her mystique.

To anyone's knowledge none had seen her outside the
palace walls since the invasion of the Christian crusaders in
1096 AD.

Regardless of her physical absence, her reach was
long, probing, and unyielding. Her influence felt by all
worldwide, and her dictates were always carried out by her

special elite royal guard unit trained in ways of death and destruction one could only imagine. She had part of that group with her now. No one was sure what she was capable of doing alone.

Her being here on this day was an omen for those wavering in their devotion to the current sitting council and those unhappy with the direction the council was trying to take the nation on this side of the Atlantic.

There were rumors of a movement to stage a coup and separate from the others around the globe rippling through the underground of the Vampire Nation. Some were willing to start a war to be able to come out of the shadows.

Any sane vampire knew for such an action to take place, vampire supremacy would have to be the end goal and total world domination as the by-product. Anything less would simply result in their persecution. There were six billion people on the planet. As a race, they were vastly outnumbered. Regardless of the fact they were genetically superior and physically powerful, they were not indestructible.

The sea of bodies parted. As recognition began to dawn, the ripple of a murmur began to go out in front of her. The queen was in their midst. The mass of bodies started to drop to their knees, placing their foreheads on the cave floor in humble submission. Those who did not because of being so mesmerized by her charisma were pulled down by those who understood what was taking place.

Few took notice of the royal guard unit trailing behind her. These men were too scary to look upon even for those who still had the presence of mind to see them. Her guards were invisible, overpowered by the queen's sheer presence.

"Your Majesty this is a noteworthy surprise." The high councilman was not bowing, making the bold move to address Caroline first. Slade and Chase exchanged glances under the face shields that hid their true identity.

Caroline snubbed him, not even looking his direction as she refused to answer. It was the equivalent of refusing to shake someone's hand that had extended theirs in an offering.

Had she acknowledged him it would have sent an unspoken message that he was her equal.

That was not about to happen.

She had just shown the gathering that he was less significant to her than a slave. Instead, Caroline inclined her head in acknowledgment to the supreme justice of the Council of Judges. Her manner to the judge was one of favor, very friendly and familiar. "Justice Savoto, I am happy to see you again, after so many years. How are the girls?"

"Well, thank you for asking, Majesty."

Caroline had fostered all three of the justice's daughters at court and masterfully engaged them in activities that garnered them excellent mates from excellent bloodlines. The justice was in the queen's debt on a personal level.

Only after speaking to each judge, in turn, did Caroline address the high councilman with no preliminary pleasantry. Another sign she was unhappy.

"I have come for the hollaquine. Turn her over to my guards immediately," Caroline said with little fanfare.

Slade being an expert in body language could easily detect that the high councilman was seething at the perceived audacity of this monarch. To think she could simply show up here in the Americas after nine hundred years of an autonomous rule made his blood boil. That made him, even more, a dangerous foe.

"I do not have her; therefore, it is not possible," the councilman said as Caroline sauntered up the steps one at a time with her entourage following close at hand.

Chase and Slade were on either side of her, prepared to defend her if necessary. She was their ticket out.

"Oh, but I think it is very possible. Playing word games with me is never a smart move. You are not old enough or smart enough to pull it off with any finesse. You should know your place, Levi. Now, be a good boy, and sit back down in your little chair."

Slade wondered just how far Caroline would be able to push the councilman until his ego got the better of any common sense he had left.

Perhaps that is her plan, he thought.

"Levi, Levi, Levi." Caroline shook her head and sighed dramatically for impact. Calling him by his first name in front of all the commoners showed she was refusing to allow him to feel superior or even close to her equal in his title as high councilman. "I am most displeased with you, but you would not know that would you? You have refused the last two summonses. I felt you were dead, or there must be something here so engaging that you felt it necessary to defy your queen. And now you think to defy me to my face. I'm disappointed, Levi." Sophia eased up beside her and whispered in her ear. "The one they call Thomas Levine, bring him. I *know* you have him under your authority."

Slade felt the council's personal guard moving through the crowd and circling in behind them. They were willing to risk life and limb to protect a member of their race who had set himself up as a little king in his kingdom.

Slade could see that the councilman never dreamed Caroline would ever think to come to the Americas. She probably wouldn't have had Sophia not summoned her with the urgent message of what was happening here.

Now, the big, bad she-wolf was back, and the councilman was thinking to take them by surprise. That wasn't happening. They would be ready.

Chase and Slade cautiously pulled out the guns loaded with the lethal bullets, hiding them in the folds of the royal guard uniform cloaks they wore.

Was Levine waiting in the shadows, watching the events unfold? Was the queen's presence a complication for Levine? Slade wondered. Probably, but from Levine's perspective probably not completely unwelcome. Slade could see Levine working with it. If he could kill or have the crowd capture her, then Levine's plan of world domination would be even easier.

Slade felt Yalena close as the fine hair on his neck stood. His blood quickened in his veins.

She is in this very room, he thought, narrowing his focus and scanning the room.

There in the deepest shadows, he saw Yalena and Kristen as her aura became visible as a beacon in the fog. Yuri was standing by Levine's side with Kristen held in restraints. Yalena was on Yuri's left as they crouched in the shadows.

"Kristen." He spoke her name without thinking of the acute hearing of the old ones. The queen and councilman both swiftly turned to look at him.

Slade rushed off the podium with Chase only a step behind. Pandemonium erupted all around them as screams filled the air, and the crowd began to scatter, seeking shelter from the weapons' fire that the councilman's guards had foolishly unleashed.

Slade and Chase followed suit.

Caroline issued one order, and except Sophia and the master guard, the remainder of her royal guard rushed forward to assist.

Slade, with Chase's help, masterfully cleared a path to Kristen just before Yuri tried to escape with her. Slade spun him around and blocked his way before he could escape down a hidden tunnel. This man had dared to drink from his woman. If they came out of this alive, Yuri would be the first to pay.

"Going somewhere?" Slade asked, expertly placing the silver blade to Yuri's jugular. "Let—Her—Go. I won't ask again."

Yuri looked around for any help that might be coming. There was none. They cut the councilman's guards down before they could advance, being no match for the royal guard, the lethal bullets in Chase's gun, or the wooden arrows unleashed from the bow Sophia wielded with perfection and skill matched only by a master archer.

The queen's guards moved so fast that Levine never saw them coming. "I have never seen anything like it. I'm impressed. I need to investigate what sort of genetic anomaly was present to create these superfighters. With such a force behind me, I would never be touched."

Pulled out of hiding away from his circle of protection, Levine was pushed to the platform forcing him to come face-to-face with the Queen.

"Sophia, is this the man?" Caroline asked softly.

"Yes, Your Majesty. He is the one," Sophia acknowledged the queen's question.

"I am slightly curious as to why you have requested this method of restitution. Going to the Council of Violations would have been much safer."

"We are vampires, Your Majesty. Nothing we do is safe or sedate."

Caroline nodded. "Point taken. Nevertheless, if you wish to do this, so be it. It is neither here nor there to me as your queen. Name your terms for Levine's death, Sophia," the queen announced and at the same time turned around to the high councilman who had stood up, coming from behind to protest. "Sit down!" Caroline pointed at him and ordered with enough authority that he dare not defy her.

Levine laughed at Sophia. "Am I to assume this is an old-fashioned indemnity match?"

"Yes," Sophia answered with a single monotone syllable.

"This young vampire is no match for me," he gloated. I am almost as strong as the vampire, and I'm certainly more cunning."

Levine slowly walked up beside Sophia. Slade was looking for any signs that Levine might recognize her. He did not. She meant nothing to him.

"You feel I have wronged you when I do not even know you?" Levine looked at the high councilman for intervention. "I protest my innocence. I have never hurt this woman."

Sophia was face-to-face with the one responsible for who she was, and he had no recollection of the hell he had caused. "You have no idea of the wrong you have caused my family and me."

"You bring no evidence of this wrong." The councilman was swift in his decision. "The council agrees with the general. You are free to go, General Levine."

Slade watched as the high councilman waved Levine away, quick to agree just to get Levine out of the area. Levine could very quickly make a bad situation entirely unsalvageable and had become a liability to his cause.

Slade stepped up. "Not—so—fast. I bring the case before the council. He has wronged me, and I'm sure you remember who I am." Slade pulled off the helmet.

"And where he goes, I go." Chase pulled off his helmet as well. The ripple of excitement was tangible as it raced through the crowd.

The arena was set between the supernatural and the mortal. The clapping and cheers were defining. The gathering had just gotten exciting. Few there realized this was no staged match for entertainment, but a real fight to the death. Those that did see it for the truth felt their fangs tingle in excitement.

Levine narrowed his eyes. The mortal and the shifter had played right into his hands. "If I kill any of them, then my prize will be the hollaquine."

"Done," said the councilman.

The councilman had just sealed his fate in Slade's mind. There was no doubt in anyone's mind that Levine and the councilman were somehow in this together. Slade was not clear who led who down this path of self-destruction. It did not matter. They were both guilty.

And, before anyone could protest the terms, the battle for Kristen's life had begun. There was nothing Slade could do to counter.

Chapter 17

The crowd made a ring around the fighters and money was changing hands. A deadly dance began as Levine taunted them.

"I got to screw her before all my soldiers tasted her, shifter."

Slade was not falling for it as he went on the offensive, lunging quickly at Levine and getting in the first shot.

Gasps and cheers escaped the crowd. Most never dreamed this shifter could best this great general who was legendary in battle. Chase followed quickly, cutting and slashing any and all flesh he could find. Levine was not a vampire and damaged more easily, but he healed at lightning speed.

Unless the flesh was severed from the bone, cuts instantly knitted back together. Sophia got in even closer, ripping and tearing flesh from bone. Levine managed to get a hand on her and in one mighty snap pulled her arm from its socket, rendering it useless as it dangled at her side.

That did not stop her. She fought like a woman possessed.

The battle raged on, and Levine was losing to Sophia regardless of the fact he was damaging her beyond repair. She was tearing him apart one small piece at a time, unrelenting and on a mission with a single purpose.

Chase and Slade backed her up, evening the odds when the fight became one-sided. This battle was her fight as much as Slade's. If she could not finish it, Slade and Chase would.

Sophia had confided in Chase and then filed a formal grievance with the queen stating how Levine had taken her from work one evening.

For their amusement, he had let his soldiers brutally rape and drink from her to the point she had almost died. Levine had left her for dead never realizing that she had already begun the transformation from human to vampire.

Sophia had wasted away in agony for six days while her body slowly ate itself up on the inside. Without comfort, she suffered alone in filth and vomit. Her polluted blood boiled her alive from the inside out. It was a miracle she even survived and did not become an even viler creature. Those who did not gracefully make the conversion the council judged and killed if caught, because they became known as the flesh eaters.

The flesh eaters had no higher brain function and ran purely on instinct. They had no emotions, were killing machines, and lived on the flesh of the dead. Their stench was so foul that the aroma had been known to strangle a man, rendering him unconscious. The eater would then delight in him, slowly eating him alive as a delicacy seldom savored.

Sophia was prepared to testify before the assembly how she had sought Levine out after she was strong enough and begged for his help. His price for that support was the forced abandonment of her children.

At first, she refused to leave them until Levine had locked her and her children up in a room. For three days Sophia had endured the burn of the blood thirst before finally succumbing to the untamed and wild beast within her.

Sophia killed her son after the third day when as a newly formed vampire the blood thirst took control.

She had been horrified and begged Levine to take her daughter away before she killed her too.

Levine did as she asked.

Sophia had not placed stipulations on the request, and Levine dumped the girl into the streets. Levine had left Sophia's remaining child without any means of support, and the child had turned to drugs and prostitution to survive as a young teen.

That child was Kristen's mother.

Slade had nearly come unhinged, understanding that Levine's sin against Sophia had for three generations wreaked havoc. Kristen would never have been savagely raped by her mother's pimp if he had left Sophia alone. Slade felt it a personal affront to him as Kristen's mate.

If Sophia couldn't finish this fight to avenge her, her daughter, and granddaughter, then he would as Kristen's mate. Levine was not walking out of this ring alive unless he, Chase, and Sophia were already dead.

Even then, Caroline had vowed to finish it.

Chase and Slade felt Sophia faltering as Levine dealt her a deathblow. Shredded and bleeding Sophia continued to fight to the bitter end. Slade pulled her to safety and out of harm's way.

If Chase could have made Levine suffer more, he would have and gladly. As it was, Chase and Slade cut him over and over until Levine threatened Kristen one time too many. Chase had heard enough and took the role of executioner upon himself, feeling Kristen would not understand Slade's violent behavior toward Levine, no matter if justified.

Slade jumped back into the ring of death just as Chase cleaved Levine through the left shoulder from neck to right hip, basically severing him in two. Attuned to each other, they worked as a unit, and with a mighty shove, the two men pushed Levine into the flesh eater's pit below. All could hear his screams.

Levine was still alive when the flesh eaters, who the vampires kept for disposals such as this, consumed him.

This race believed in cleaning up after themselves and taking out their trash.

Evidence was something the vampire never left behind. Levine had violated that law when he left Sophia for dead.

The Council of Judgments convicted Levine of the crime of littering.

In the vampire world, that was a death sentence.

Chase and Slade merely carried it out.

Chapter 18

Slade gently picked up the dying Sophia and took her to the bottom of the steps of the platform. She had fought bravely in the face of adversity and deserved the honor of a swift death. Anything else would be inhumane. It would take her weeks, even months, to die.

What she did next shocked them all.

"By my rights as the victor, I claim the healer as mine for as long as I exist on this earth." Sophia's broken and bloody body ached for eternal release. She was never meant to be a creature of Levine's cruel making. "I claim the healer as my prize." Her whisper was audible in the cavernous room as a total deathly stillness settled.

The whole of the colony did not make a sound as it collectively held its breath. Sophia's words echoed off the limestone walls carved from millions of years of groundwater seeping through the crevices as if the very stone were crying.

"Sophia, no!" Kristen screamed, rushing for Slade. "No! Slade?" Kristen understood what that would mean.

In the heat of the battle, everyone had forgotten Yuri. He grabbed Kristen as she tried to reach past him to get to Slade. The beast took Kristen and in a mad rage tossed her backward so fast none could react to his quickness.

Kristen hit the cavern wall with a resounding crack, and her body slid to crumble at the base of the rock. That act earned Yuri a date with the devil as Slade moved with lightning speed, dual swords on either side of Yuri's throat. In unison, those blades crossed, severing flesh, cleaving bone, tendons, and spine. Yuri's head rolled, and his body crumpled to the ground in an ooze of dark-green and black goo, which bubbled and glistened in the torchlight.

Slade stepped over what was left of Yuri and moved forward, wiping the blackened, corrosive blood off his swords. He dared not touch any living tissue with the vile and toxic residue.

"Kristen? Oh, God, baby, talk to me," he begged. Her near-lifeless body hung limply in his arms as he picked her up and rushed forward to the platform. He could not heal her. Not without permission.

If only I had not touched her, he thought as he prayed silently for the mercy of this court.

"Please, let me save her, let me heal her, and I shall serve out my sentence in the host." He humbled himself

234

before the council, who he knew could say no more quickly than yes.

He was prepared to die to save Kristen, and this was the only way.

The high councilor narrowed his eyes.

Was he still set on his plan working, regardless of the mess Levine and his clowns had made? Slade wondered. *Did he think that this fiasco still had not touched him? Did he believe that he had a way to have both the healer and the hollaquine to do his bidding?* It would appear so.

The councilman turned to the panel of judges "They are both guilty of a grave offense, Justice Savoto. She must die, and he is ours as a healer."

The councilman's pretense to a hard-line approach and his effort not to appear to relent too quickly was his way of keeping Slade from seeing through his plan.

It failed.

The councilman was not about to let his prize go. Slade and the others realized that Kristen's blood was what the councilman needed to raise his army. Levine was certainly replaceable.

Slade had done his homework. Now, he prayed it would pay off. "I protest our guilt under the Law of Extinction, Your Honor." Slade addressed the supreme justice of the Council of Judgments bypassing the Council of Violations altogether. The councilman had already rendered a verdict to the judges.

In Slade's legal opinion it was now an appeal.

"I did what I did because she is one of a kind, Your Honor. Under the Law of Extinction, I am allowed to heal in the event of a dire emergency or if the loss of life is imminent, regardless of the fact the life is not a vampire."

"That's ridiculous!" The councilman scoffed at the idea. "It is ludicrous for anyone to think that simply any life was as important as a vampire's life."

The supreme justice calmly corrected him. "Not as ridiculous as you might think, Councilman Levi. The law set by the wizard's Council of Nine is universal to all mystic creatures and not the law of the Vampire Nation. Therefore, Councilman, it supersedes our laws. I must confer with the other judges before rendering my decision," the supreme justice interjected.

"Damn," the high councilman said.

Slade had trumped him.

They all watched as the Council of Judgments put their heads together. The whole of the chamber was holding its breath as the low murmur of the judge's voices buzzed softly.

The supreme justice turned back to the crowd. "The healer is right, High Councilman, and the whole of the Council of Judgments concurs. There was no violation of the law."

"He healed his mate. It is forbidden, and that *is* vampire law."

His comment made it apparent that he was grappling for anything to pin on Slade to control Slade's destiny. Slade was quick to think on his feet.

"I healed her before I bonded with her, Your Honor. There is no break in the law. She is innocent. Let me heal her now even though I am her mate. She is still one of a kind, so the Law of Extinction still applies. I am asking permission out of respect for the court. Let her live, and let her go. If you refuse my request, I will heal her nevertheless and formally call and request mediation with the Council of Nine and the wizard's tribunal to arbitrate her release."

"Wait, let's not be hasty here." Justice Savoto held up a restraining hand. "I have not yet ruled unfavorably to your cause."

None wanted the wizards involved. Their attendance would only result in one thing; extreme punishment brought on by the Vampire Nation's actions.

A visit from the wizards today would not bode well for the vampires any more than it had in the past. The nation had been left to their devices for too long, in Slade's opinion, and had for centuries been pushing the line of civil and proper behavior further out of bounds. Levine was an example.

Anyone who knows how the vampire system works understands that it is not the place of the Council of Judgments to change this behavior. It is the Council of Violations place to bring charges against the conduct that breaches the laws.

The Council of Judgment's place is to judge once the Council of Violation levels charges. Not that the judges agreed with the direction the nation had wandered. It was just not their place to point out they were heading further into dicey, treacherous waters that would eventually gain the notice of the wizards or worse, the humans.

Here in the New World with this high councilor at the head of the Council of Violations, the charges for such behavior had been fewer and fewer as the centuries rolled along. It was becoming quickly and very transparently visible to the queen and judges that his corruption was boundless.

Queen Caroline had stayed in the Old World at the seat of her power when the great migration began during the Spanish Inquisition. She remained blissfully ignorant of the actions here in the New World.

Caroline's advisers keeping her in the dark for personal reasons did not help. Her showing up for this gathering was quite a surprise, and it had opened the queen's eyes to a few things that were long overdue for a change. If the expression on her face was any indication, then the supreme justice was happy to see the queen finally take notice.

"Very well. I seem to have no other choice except to rescind my charges against the two of you in the healing violation of a nonvampire. If Supreme Justice Savoto agrees, then you may heal her. However, you belong to me, not Sophia. She is not of the line of Cain. I am Cain's descendant and next in line for a healer."

"He is mine!" Yalena protested from the audience. "I tasted him first." Then she realized what she had said. She had not asked for permission to taste the pure blood of the healer.

The color drained from her face as she saw the anger come over the face of the high councilman, and she fell to her knees, crouching in fear, begging for the mercy of the court for her misstep.

"You dare disobey a directive of the council? You dare to taste what is forbidden to you and belongs only to those born to the highest caste of vampire lineage? Never forget that I am your creator. I made you, Yalena! You were not born vampire, and, as such, are no better than a dog. Still you savored the blood of the ancients' gift to us of the high caste? You should have claimed him outright and taken your chances to fight for that privilege as Sophia has tried unsuccessfully to do. It was a grave mistake." He turned to his guards. "Take her to the inner chamber caves and chain her there. She is to be allowed to eat only during the full and total eclipse of the sun as it passes overhead here in the desert."

Slade watched Caroline in fascination. Her assessment of this proceeding was obviously an eye opener, and unless he missed his guess the infractions and behavior she was witnessing would be quickly rectified. It had to be swift and brutally just. It had to be so for the sake of the nation. Men such as Levi were a danger to the vampire's very existence and way of life. She would deal with him on her terms. Slade felt confident.

The Council of Judgments sat up in their chairs at the bold and unilateral move they had just witnessed from the high councilman. None saw fault with the swift judgment or sentence, only in the fact the councilman acted unilaterally. The Council of Violations was only to bring charges and witnesses before the judges. The Council of Violations' job was to present facts, not to deliver or dispense justice.

That was Justice Savoto's job and had been for eighteen hundred years.

Supreme Justice Savoto spoke while never taking her eyes off the high councilman.

"You may heal her, shifter." Then she turned to Yalena and said, "And, as to you, so it is written, so it shall be carried out." The gavel came down.

"No!" Yalena screamed. "No!" She fought, digging in her heels. "I beg the indulgence and forgiveness of the judges. I beg you! Nooooooo!"

The back chamber door slammed shut on her screams, leaving the assembly room eerily quiet as the audience stared at the lone shoe left behind just inside the doorway. It had come off in her struggle and was the only testimony to the fate she would now endure.

Everyone there who was vampire understood what the sentence meant. She would be kept totally in the dark, all senses deprived, and she would slowly go insane from the hunger. She would become so emaciated that she would not have the strength or ability to blood feed, even when the sun eclipsed. Here in this spot of the desert, it came only once every three hundred and seventy-three years and gone in less than seven minutes. She would feel the burn of the blood thirst forever never being able to sate it. She would never die.

It was the radiation from the sun that slowly killed them and forced them through the ages to become creatures of the night to slow the process. In only two exceptions could one escape the sun's effects: the depths of the ocean or in a cave where it did not matter if it was night or day. Locked into the depths of the cave no radiation would ever touch her. Her sentence was nearly eternal.

It was truly their hell on earth.

~*****~

Caroline watched as Slade laid Kristen's body down on the platform in front of the court. She was barely alive, broken and bleeding inside and out. Taking her face into his hands, he softly kissed her lips.

Chase stood behind her, and she reached around to take his hand, squeezing it hard enough to break his bones. This tenderness exhibited between the shifter and his mate totally enthralled her.

Caroline felt something stir deep in her core at the sight of one willing to give so much for the life of another. It was not entirely foreign to her, and this show of self-sacrifice touched her in a place she felt come back to life.

Slade began to shimmer, and the gasps filled the chamber as the bodies pressed forward to see. None of them had ever seen a healer before. The vampires closely guarded the healer's presence and existence through the ages. They were given only to those of the highest rank of the highest caste. The healers were given only to those born in the lineage of Cain, who was their maker and first of their kind.

The chamber breathed in unison as ten thousand stood there, transfixed on the altar, watching the prone shape there. Time stood still, and none dared to move as Slade disappeared.

Chapter 19

Kristen slowly regained consciousness. He did not erase her memory of this blending, and he left pieces of himself behind. He wanted her to remember him being inside her and hoped by leaving something behind that he would be able to keep his memories alive, too.

Slade was shocked, awed, and humbled. Kristen was pregnant from the bonding. He touched his baby. She was so tiny and vulnerable. Blending with her, he infused her with powerful enzymes to help increase the flow of blood to her developing cells and to help stop her life from ebbing away. She was growing at an astounding rate. He had just made love to Kristen less than twenty-four hours ago. This child would be born in a matter of a few weeks. He would never know her. His grief was sharp with that knowledge.

He wanted Kristen and his child to have the feeling of their closeness past this breaking dawn.

"I remember," she whispered. "You touched me and healed me before. Don't leave me, Slade."

He took her hand and kissed it tenderly. "I will always be with you. You carry my child, Kristen, and I shall never forget."

He turned from Kristen and faced the Council of Violations.

"I know what you are thinking, High Councilman." His baby was empathic, and she saw what was in the councilman's mind and the blackness of his heart. She had shared her knowledge with Slade as he swept through her blood and her developing mind. Slade had felt her fear of dying and her fear of living as a captive of this cruel creature.

Slade would never let that happen.

"You wish to deceive the Queen and this court, Councilman. Do so and, God as my witness, I shall find a way to kill you. Under the conditions of the Treaty of The Children of the Sun, I vow to annihilate you if you so much as think to touch my friends, my mate, or my offspring."

"Don't think to threaten me, shifter." He shot to his feet. The violence was shimmering just beneath the surface, and it rolled over the crowd, eliciting gasps of fear and terror. This vampire was ancient and powerful from a millennium of feeding off the most stalwart warriors from around the world and perfecting his art of deception and deceit.

Slade was stronger than the councilman. Light, goodness, and a resolve hard and tempered like steel born of fire filled him

Slade stepped closer. He was unafraid and undeterred. He would not cower in the presence of this evil. "It is no threat, Councilman. Do not think to break the Law of Mass Creation. Do not dare to use Kristen's blood or the blood of my child, whether unborn or born, as a means to build your army. If you do, then, as the one wronged, I sentence you in advance to the depths of the Mariana Trench, chained and weighted to the bottom for all eternity."

The comments that traveled around the room were audible. The anticipation was thick.

"You have no teeth to your words, shifter. You have no proof." The councilman was standing and acting alone in his deceit and failed to recognize the others of the Council of Violations and Council of Judgments had stepped away from him, disassociating themselves from his treasonous actions.

"I don't need any proof. I have three things on my side; the others, the law, and the queen."

Led by Bobby and Samantha, the room began to fill with the other creatures that had taken the abuse and behavior of this council for long enough. The numbers were overwhelming, now that they had finally banded together after so many years as fragmented cells.

The council had only two choices: relent or defy the queen, and the result would be civil war.

Slade stared the councilman down. He would never blink first. "You shall never break the laws of this treaty from this point forward lest I bring the wrath of God and the wizards down upon you. Supreme Justice Savoto, I request an immediate verdict."

The supreme justice saw no other alternative than to render immediate judgment in the case of the Children of the Sun versus the Vampire Nation. The law was on Slade's side. The Children of the Sun, those Native Americans with the bloodline of the healer, had finally challenged the vampire behavior and the way they had breached the treaty for so long. Finally standing up to them, and justifiably so, she just wondered why it had taken so long to do so.

"Shifter, these bold and aggressive maneuvers have earned the respect of this justice. You shall be the last healer gifted to the race. You are willingly doing this?"

"Yes, my life for Kristen's. That was the agreement."

"So it shall be written, so it shall be carried out. Now, your sentence is to commence immediately." The gavel came down with a sound that rendered a feeling of finality.

"Slade, no! There has to be another way. There has to be another way!" Kristen wept. "Slade…"

He kissed her one final time. "If only things had been different…"

Slade knelt down beside Sophia and began the ritual, never taking his eyes off Kristen. He wanted her face to be the last thing he remembered before fading into Sophia.

Halfway through, Sophia cried the words no one had ever heard in ten thousand years.

"I release you, healer! Come forth and live free."

"No!" The high councilman rose to his feet. "Kill her before he emerges," he ordered, pointing at Sophia's body. He knew if he killed the host before Slade fully emerged, Slade would have to find another host quickly or die as well. He could never let such a prize go free. "Kill her!"

"No one move!" Chase had Queen Caroline by her hair, the silver blade at her throat. "Touch any of us and the little bitch gets it and you," Chase inclined his head to the high councilman, "you double-crossing pile of dog vomit will be next," he vowed. "Hear me?"

"Nobody move and do as he says!" Queen Caroline ordered. No one had to know that she had made that pact with Chase to flush out the one who had been undermining her control and secretly trying to overtake her position as regent.

This action by the councilman was unquestionably a serious plot but not the one she had hoped to uncover. She was secretly pleased. Chase would still have to come to her aid. It was a gamble. She knew that Chase did not give a shit about that pact. He had never promised not to kill her. He had contracted to find the person who was trying to kill her. Two very different things.

"Nobody move," Chase repeated, pulling Caroline back against him just a little tighter. "Or I'll cleanly and openly before God and all you blood-loving bastards slit her throat, no matter how beautiful that throat might be."

The crowd did not dare risk moving. Caroline was their queen who was in danger. No one doubted Chase's statement, not even Caroline, after seeing what he and Slade did to Levine and several of his men.

Caroline felt it was nothing short of what the bastards deserved, and she noted that many in the crowd had stopped those who had tried to interfere. Even if they were vampire they had their limits on cruelty, and Levine had disgraced them and brought shame and death to his house. His actions had almost cost them their ability to continue operations in the relative secrecy they had enjoyed for millennia.

Their operations here in the Southwest were lucrative. Minerals were the state's richest natural resource, and New Mexico, being one of the US leaders in the output of uranium and potassium salts, petroleum, natural gas, copper, gold, silver, zinc, lead, and molybdenum, also contributes heavily to their income.

The principal manufacturing industries included food products, chemicals, transportation equipment, lumber, electrical machinery, and stone, clay, and glass products. More than two-thirds of New Mexico's farm income came from livestock products, especially sheep. Cotton, pecans, and sorghum were the most important field crops. Corn, peanuts, beans, onions, chilies, and lettuce were also grown. They had their hands in all of it, funneling millions each year into the coffers.

Chase and Slade just saved them the trial. Some of the more conservative members of the nation felt Chase and Slade's actions toward Levine were simply judgment and admired this human and shifter for their ability to best one of their older and more powerful generals. That action they could respect.

This group of individuals showed no fear of them, regardless of the fact the humans were less powerful than their vampire adversaries. Also, something the vampire could respect. The fact the two men had allowed Sophia to exact her revenge, even knowing she could die to do it, was something they could relate. It was unexpected from the humans.

Slade rolled off Sophia, instantly taking on his physical form. She was dying, and it had not totally been an unselfish act to release him. Vampire or not, the very act of freeing him had also freed her.

The vampire were programmed never to take one's life; this was the only way to gain her freedom.

Kristen ran to Sophia and knelt by her side, holding her hand. "Sophia, thank you."

"Kristen, you are my flesh and the only evidence I ever existed. And contrary to what Chase may think, I still have some of my humanity remaining."

Sophia died that day and finally gained the only true eternal life that she had ever really wanted.

Chapter 20

Caroline guaranteed safe passage no matter where they were in the world by making it known around the globe that Chase, Slade, and his group were in her high favor. None dared to defy her after the display of the very public and very nasty execution of the high councilor.

The word had circled the globe through the underground networks with lightning speed. Cell phones and e-mail did not hurt either to get the word spread.

Caroline had made it abundantly clear that she was not happy with the leadership and fully placed the blame for the bad behavior of this group on Levine and Levi. Those who swore immediate fealty to the crown and those who were forcibly drawn in by intimidation or threat Caroline immediately pardoned. Those who resisted were noted and carefully monitored.

It was a brilliant move.

She had demonstrated her power to destroy any opposition or uprising yet garnered the love of those who thought their world was surely coming to an end. They knew there would be no second chance for mercy. This grace period was their one warning shot over the bow.

Caroline would not be taking her eye off this group anytime soon. Slade and Chase weren't either. They stayed behind with Caroline for several months. They didn't do the dirty work. The judges did that. Instead, they became bounty hunters, or more formally called a Queen's Enforcer bringing the accused to the queen for trial. Those who were still loyal to the cause of Levi and Levine would never have that option again.

Slade and Chase reduced the Vampire Nation by several hundred over the last few months. The flesh eaters would not be hungry for a decade.

There were several good things to come from the encounter in the caves and the offer of help to the queen. The cash that infused the coffers of McKinnon-Bride Personal Security was not as welcome as the relief of knowing anyone who had helped Levine and Levi were dead or neutralized to the point of no longer being a threat.

Slade was sleeping better at night because of it, too.

Chapter 21

September 6, 2007

Slade took Kristen by the hand and before God and fifty witnesses married her. For better or worse, richer or poorer, he was happy to call her his wife.

"I guess you know I have to move in with you," Slade teased as they danced at the reception. "I'm a homeless bum without a job."

He had sold his home months ago, and with the bounty hunter duties officially at an end, he was unemployed.

Kristen pressed her cheek to his. "And yet, I'll still take you. I need a pool boy," she whispered close to his ear.

"Cool! I'll take that job if it's available," Chase spoke up, dancing with Eden in his arms. The baby girl was having almost as much fun as he was.

"Shut up, Chase," Slade laughed. "That job's taken."

Robert waltzed up next to the dancing couple. He had his lovely wife Katherine on his arm."Well, how are you going to do that and work off the plane you crashed and burned? It wasn't insured, you know. I could sure use your skills at McKinnon-Bride, Slade. The job here in Dallas is yours if you want to give the pool job to Chase."

"What job?" Kristen asked, surprised by this sudden turn.

"Did you bring the wedding gift for her? That was the deal to accept the position," Slade asked cryptically.

"Yeah. Over there." Robert tilted his head to the left.

Kristen's and Slade's eyes followed his direction.

Standing awkwardly in the doorway was a striking young man in a sharply pressed Marine Corps dress-blue uniform.

Kristen looked back at Slade with a look of bewilderment crossing her face.

"Stephen," he said.

"Stephen?" Kristen whispered, almost not believing her eyes. "Stephen!" She ran to him, pushing her way through the couples on the dance floor. "Oh God! Oh God, Stephen, is it really you?"

Stephen took her into his arms and held on for dear life.

"Slade and Mr. McKinnon said you never stopped looking for me," he confessed.

"I thought for sure that I had lost you forever." She held him tightly, fearful it was just a dream.

The young man smiled. "I never forgot you or your face. I just forgot who I was. I was one of the lucky ones. A good family adopted me."

"Oh, that's wonderful. I was so afraid that you got lost in the system. I'm so happy for you, Stephen!"

"My name is Shane Sullivan now, Krisy."

"Krisy?" she questioned. "Oh, my God, that's right. That is what you used to call me." She turned to her husband and threw her arms around his neck. "You did this for me? Thank you, thank you, thank you, Slade." She turned him loose and went to Robert. "Thank you, Robert," she said, kissing him on the cheek.

Slade smiled indulgently. "Neither of us can take credit. Kari did this for you, Kris. I just followed through with her wishes."

Kristen could have asked for the world, and if possible, Slade would have delivered. He felt confident this was a far better gift to receive. Stephen was family, and Slade felt there was no greater gift as he looked at his growing family.

"How? How did you find him?" she asked, looking back and forth between the two men who, second only to her child, were the most important thing in the world to her.

Along with the three million dollars, Kari left instructions for Slade to run a national campaign to find Stephen using the one thing that broke it wide open.

The camera memory card Kari had left for him in that plastic baggy didn't contain any damning evidence as they first thought. It had contained the same family photo of Kristen and Stephen as kids that he pulled from her desk while in Kristen's office.

Slade pulled out that photocopy of the picture to show her. He had paid handsomely to have the image of Stephen aged and then had it broadcast far and wide on every media outlet he could afford from Anchorage to Zurich. Twenty-four hours after launching that campaign, Slade got the call from Marine Master Sergeant Felix Ramirez from Camp Pendleton in California.

Sergeant Shane Stephen Ransom Sullivan had finally come home.

Chapter 22

Dallas, Texas
September 27, 2007

Caroline and Chase closed the door to Kristen's study for one final negotiation on the finer points of the agreement that they struck in the cave.

There had simply not been enough time back at the gathering to hammer out details, and they both conceded that point. There had been few opportunities to meet with Caroline since the events in New Mexico because of the grueling pace he and Chase kept in flushing out and finding the violators all around the globe. And no time to discuss the contract.

This meeting was the first time Chase found himself alone with Caroline since he was twenty-three years old.

More precisely this was the first time Chase had *allowed* them to be alone since that day he walked away from her in the desert.

Caroline stood up stating that she had pressing matters to attend. "I think the terms are fair. I will summon you when I am ready for your services."

That flew all over Chase. "I will not be summoned, Caroline. I'm not one of your night-crawling subjects. Call me, and I'll carry out my duties to you as an official employee and representative of McKinnon-Bride Personal Security. This is business, babe, no pleasure about it."

"Oh, Chase. You are such a serious puss." Caroline waved him off.

"The final contract will be in the mail, Caroline. Sign it or don't sign it. I don't give a shit one way or the other. However, I will not lift a finger until you do."

"Very well, I'll be in touch." She smiled and left the room.

Chase fell into the closest chair, shaking his head.

"What the hell have I done?" he asked himself, knowing this could be a death sentence for him to venture so deeply into the bowels of the vampire court.

If I die it will be for a good cause, he thought as he pushed out of the chair and went to see the reason he risked life and limb in the first place. It was in his DNA to protect the innocent.

Slade and Kristen's baby girl, Eden, was in the nursery. He went to see her every chance he could. He had to go ever chance he could. She was growing so fast that the changes were astounding each time he saw her. Now, he would simply have to wait for the call, but for how long?

Only Caroline could answer that question.

###

Contact the Author

Please visit Ranay James on Facebook:
http://www.facebook.com/pages/Ranay-
James/441095109282762

Join The James Gang Newsletter
http://ow.ly/tTIqH

Twitter
https://twitter.com/ranayjames

Email Me
info@ranayjames.com

Google+
http://goo.gl/KcsKNx

About The Author

Ranay James moved to a small farm in East Texas along with her husband and two dogs after walking away from the fast-paced corporate life in 2012.

Ranay graduated from college majoring in accounting and finance with a minor in business management and law.

Becoming a romance writer seems a most unlikely path for a woman who spent most of her career managing people and operational practices within the corporate environment.

It all began in 2004 on New Year's Day. Having made a list of things that she wanted to accomplish for the year, she added some items to that list that would push her skill set and take her out of her comfort zone. Learning to speak Spanish and write a novel were the two items that she felt would stretch her abilities the most, having no prior training in either. Later that day, Ranay sat down at her computer. Looking at that blank Word document, she wrote the first thing that came into her mind.

"What were you thinking?" she wrote, having remembered the line from a dream she had in a hotel room in Houston, Texas in 2002. Several chapters in, Ranay found her voice as the story began to form. It poured out from a place that she never knew existed. Ranay began to write that day in 2004 and simply never stopped.

With twelve published works to her name and nine more completed awaiting publication, Ranay has found a new passion—the love of storytelling and sharing her characters with the world.